CHAOTIC APERITIFS

A HIDDEN DISHES NOVELLA

TAO WONG

Chaotic Apéritifs

A Starlit Publishing Book
Published by Starlit Publishing

PO Box 30035
High Park PO
Toronto, ON
M6P 3K0
Canada

www.starlitpublishing.com

Ebook ISBN: 9781778551710

Print ISBN: 9781778551949

Contents

Pineapple Upside Down Cake

L ight spilled out of the glowing white and yellow portal, bisecting reality with a twist of magic. On one end, a modern kitchen and a chef; on the other, open fields filled with pineapple bushes. The smell of fresh manure and plants spilled into the industrial air of the kitchen, the whirl of quiet extractor fans running moment to moment.

Mo Meng took a box of pineapples from the farmer, carefully placing it on the counter beside him. On the other side of the portal, the sun had begun to rise, highlighting the plantation in soft glowing light, a contrast to the harsh fluorescents of the kitchen.

"Fully ripe, from my own trees. We waited till they were nearly ready to fall off before we pulled them," the farmer said, the pair of tusks that jutted from his broad mouth, framed by skin the color of a ripe tomato, all signs of the ogre's eastern origins.

Not that Hiro wasn't a native of Costa Rica these days, having been born there nearly a half-century ago, after his grandparents had immigrated from Japan. More opportunities for a good life in those distant lands, even for an oni. Especially if you knew a mage who could make a glamour enchantment.

"How's the charms holding up?" Mo Meng asked. "The higher ambient Mana levels should be putting a mild strain on them already, yes?"

Hiro nodded, touching his chest where the enchanted glamour lay beneath the light white t-shirt. "Good. My grandson's could do with a recharge, though."

"Already?"

"He was chewing on it again."

Mo Meng chuckled. "You should just let me enchant the farm. It's not good for him to have to learn how to handle the fluctuating magic all the time."

"He'll be fine," Hiro said. "I was, wasn't I?'

Mo Meng shook his head but rather than reply, picked up a pineapple and sniffed it. Sour and sweet with undertones of acid in the background. Fresh and perfect. He could feel the spiky leaves digging into his fingers, the firm flesh with just a slight give that indicated its ripeness.

Perfect.

"Bring the necklace tonight. I'll charge it." Mo Meng said, glancing at the portal. Light flickered along the edges, a sign of the strain on the enchantments. "I'll bake an extra cake, too."

"You know I'll never say no to that," Hiro said, moving faster to pick up and return with two more boxes. Enough for the small batch that Mo Meng required for the restaurant. Even if it was thrice the amount it had been last year.

After all, the Nameless Restaurant was getting popular.

Much to its owner's chagrin.

The first step to producing today's dessert was prepping the pineapples. Making sure to position the compost bag close by, Mo Meng extracted the pineapples from their boxes and began slicing into them with his cleaver. The simple Chinese cleaver had a thick, heavy base on the end to give him the heft he needed to go through the tops and bottoms with ease, but was light enough that he could strip the skin from the sides with a deft twist of the hand.

His hands moved with swift efficiency, the thunk of cleaver on chopping board echoing through the empty kitchen into the open dining room. The large viewing window from the kitchen allowed Mo Meng a clear view of the empty room while he worked, a necessary addition to the kitchen when he had worked alone. That wasn't the case these days, of course.

Nowadays, it just made serving finished dishes easier.

Off-white fluorescent lights bathed the kitchen in stark illumination, allowing him to view the entirety of his domain with ease, though there were a few uncommon modifications. For one thing, though he worked with gas for the most part, the open flame grill on the left was also heated by charcoal and wood. Large, industrial extractors above the kitchen and stoves helped contain the smell, though that was further enhanced by a touch of magic.

No point in barbecuing meals over open flames and leaving his guests smelling of wood smoke. Not all of his guests would always eat the same meal, so having several options available helped. The enchantments also had the benefit of clearing the smell overnight, so that he could begin with new dishes every day and not concern himself about residual staining.

As loath as he might be to utilize magic while cooking, sometimes magical solutions just simplified things.

Once each pineapple was stripped of its thorny skin, Mo Meng utilized a new knife, slicing into the central core to pop out the hard, white nub in the middle. That part had little taste, though rather than waste it, each central nub was placed in a clear container. Later, pineapple skin and water would be added before the filled containers were set aside to create a mild organic pineapple vinegar.

In the meantime, the whole pineapple was horizontally portioned into equal-sized slices, Mo Meng keeping a running tally of the number in his mind. He placed the slices on a cooling rack, with a cookie tray underneath to catch the additional pineapple juice coming off the ripe slices. He worked silently and industriously for the most part, humming the occasional tune that came to mind, but focused on prep and the rhythmic and familiar nature of the work.

Prep, done well, was where all the real magic happened. Take your time, double-check the ingredients as they came in, make sure everything was done right. Something as simple as keeping each slice of pineapple the same width would make significant differences in the final result. Too thick, and some would cook faster than others. Too thin, and you risked burning portions of the dish.

Once done, Mo Meng made his way to the oven to begin pre-heating it. This was not a traditional home kitchen oven, but the kind used in commercial bakeries. It had multiple shelves to allow him to bake multiple cakes at the same time, and it pre-heated quickly.

For this dish, the top of the cake – or the bottom – was a mixture of brown sugar and unsalted butter. Pre-softened butter taken from the counter to simplify the mixing. Not melted, as some might recommend, which made the cake too wet for his liking. Also, Mo Meng liked to add a touch of cinnamon to the topping, the fresh spice giving an extra bite to the cake.

After adding the three ingredients to the mixing bowl, he set the bowl down and turned the mixer on, leaving it to do its work. In the meantime, he moved the newly cut pineapple slices onto kitchen paper to dry the rest of the way. The less moisture there was on the pineapples, the easier the entire mixture would set. Too much liquid and the cake would be too moist. Once that was done, buttering the square baking pans on the sides and bottom was his next task.

Checking on the creamed mixture, Mo Meng raised a spoonful of blended butter and sugar to his lips. He licked his lips, tossed the spoon aside and added a touch more sugar, his tongue tingling from the rush of pure sugar and creamed butter.

A half-dozen pans later, he took the mixing bowl and ladled out a thin layer of the sugary topping into each pan before flattening the mixture with the back of a spoon. He worked smoothly, pressing firmly as he went along, before setting the pans aside, knowing that gravity and time would fix minor mistakes.

Once done, he returned to the pineapple rings and laid them out carefully in rows of three by three, pressing gently to firmly set the rings. After that, in the pans went to the refrigerator while he worked on the cake base. The chilled pans would set the mixture, ensuring that the cake when baked would come out in a single piece.

The cake itself was the usual mixture of flour, sugar, egg and salt, with both baking powder and baking soda to help it rise. Some recipes called for a thin, dense cake layer, but Mo Meng much preferred his cakes to have some substance and size. The sweetness and tartness of the pineapple and the sugary glazed topping was better paired with a thicker cake, one with a generous dose of pineapple juice drawn from the drippings he'd gathered earlier.

Of course, that was in and of itself insufficient, and vanilla extract and a touch of nutmeg were needed to give the cake further sensory layers. Lastly, rather than milk, he preferred light whipping cream to counterbalance the density of the cake, giving it a degree of lightness that plain milk failed to offer.

Mo Meng was careful to do all this by hand rather than using the mixer, allowing him to test the consistency as he blended the cake batter. Flour overworked grew hard. The consistency became chewy rather than light and fluffy. For the same reason, he wouldn't rest the batter either when he was done.

Deep in the throes of preparation, Mo Meng barely even noticed the new presence in the kitchen. Not until the refrigerator door was opened and a blonde head started poking around at the chilling contents. Then the voice came, high and annoyed.

"No cherries?" Kelly cried out as she closed the refrigerator door.

"No. They taste horrible and I won't be adding any to my dish," Mo Meng said. Hands still holding the baking mixture, he stared at his only employee. "Also, why are you here?"

"You mean I'm fired?" Closing the door, Kelly leaned back and put a hand dramatically to her chest. "Oh, no!"

"You know what I mean. We're not opening till tonight," he said.

"You know, we should open for lunch too," Kelly said, leaning with one hip against the door. "We're so packed for dinner these days, we should probably just give people numbers before they come in."

"No numbers. No reservations. You know that," Mo Meng said, grumpily.

"I know, I know. You don't want your regulars to be blocked out," she said. "Especially the special ones."

"Exactly."

"But we've got to do something! We're beginning to get a line out there every night."

"And whose fault is that?"

"Lily's?" she ventured.

"Did the jinn put us on Google Maps?"

An unrepentant grin was his answer. Mo Meng sighed, but jerked his chin at the fridge. "Since you're here, help me out. Pull out the pans, will you?"

Pouting, Kelly did as he asked, laying each tray on the counter. Mo Meng moved along the counter, parceling out cake batter into the pans. He gently tapped the edges of each pan once he was done, to help push out any bubbles that might have formed, before he carried each pan to the oven.

A quick check verified it was pre-heated, and once he was done, he set the timer.

Kelly watched all this, arms crossed, before she spoke up. "So, pineapple upside down cake for dessert. What's the rest of the menu for today?"

Mo Meng shook his head. "You still haven't said what you're doing here."

"My job. Well, my new job. Social media. Updating socials for the new menu."

The man snorted. "I'd have texted you soon."

"Sure, but I still have to prep for tonight." A raised eyebrow was the only answer to her words. A long moment, and then Kelly's bubbly personality faded. She ducked her head. "I just needed to get out."

"Trouble at home?"

A single nod, and Mo Meng frowned.

She shook her head, cutting him off before he could ask. "No, I'm good. Just... let me hang out here a bit?"

"Of course."

Her bright smile returned and Kelly flounced out of the kitchen, leaving Mo Meng to the rest of his prep.

Social Media

Kelly threw herself into a chair near the entrance of the restaurant, the afternoon light streaming from basement windows highlighting the few tables there. She unslung the yellow purse over her shoulder onto a chair, unzipping it and pulling out a laptop. From the large purse, she also drew her cellphone, the latest Korean branded model, and grimaced at the cracked screen. She really needed to get that fixed, but she'd have to find the time. And money.

Within moments she was skimming through her social media accounts, making faces as she came across pictures of her friends. Some were still in college, true, but the majority had graduated. Office lunches, elegant and sexy – if still formal – getups. Nights out, clubbing with bottles of wine and champagne and hot guys in attendance. Claire, who was on a trip to Paris with her boyfriend, that douche.

Frustrated, she clicked off and out of her own account over to the Nameless Restaurant ones. A small smile began to light her face as pictures of the food that was served began to show up. Not from the official account, of course – the damn man kept insisting that she shouldn't take photos herself – but he hadn't barred his customers.

Not yet, at least.

Here, photos of the crème brulé that he'd done three days ago, by LadywithaBite.

There, the tomahawk steak he'd served a week ago, from HeadintheClouds.

Shelled oysters for the seafood night on Sunday, taken with a lot of close-ups but rather badly angled. However, it was probably the most popular, judging by the sheer volume of empty shells showcased by OreforYouandMe.

She was allowed to post one thing. Specifically, their menu for the day. It made her job a lot easier, since fewer people complained about the changing menu when they arrived, and how it interacted with their million and one allergies and sensitivities.

In moments, she had the menu typed out on the simple image template she'd created. She paused before submitting it, reviewing the document for typos, fighting the gut-clench of anxiety when she caught one. As she finished reading the list over twice more, her phone began to play the first notes from *Jaws*. Kelly's shoulders came up, her body hunching away from the phone before she forcibly exhaled and relaxed herself. Forced herself to reach forward and answer it.

"Yes?" She held the electronic chain slightly away from her ear as she thumbed the green icon.

"Is that how you greet your mother? I thought I taught you better?" The voice came through the phone, loud and boisterous and highly accented.

"I'm at work, Mom."

"Work? What work? You told me you work in the evenings, don't you?" her mom said incredulously. "Why are you in right now? Are you trying to become a chef? I hear they work long hours. You know what you're like when you cook, right, dear? I don't think your boss would be okay with you burning down his restaurant."

"I'm not going to burn down his restaurant," she replied. Not as if she could. Even if she was a mundane, she knew enough to know that it might take a direct strike with a missile to take down the building that housed the restaurant. Maybe not even that anymore. After Lily's last visit, Mo Meng had shut down the restaurant for three days to emplace a series of powerful new runes, not just across the restaurant itself but the building that housed it and then, later on, the entire neighborhood.

That last part, she'd only known when her regular alerts for the Nameless Restaurant and its address and cross streets – needed, due to the fact that the restaurant refused to actually pick a name – had highlighted a series of photos and a single video of ethereal nights in the neighborhood one evening.

"You say that, but then you start cooking a pot of pasta and forget about the stove..."

"I was seven!" Kelly said, hating how her voice grew whiny as she spoke. "Just... what are you looking for, Mom?"

"A mother can't call her daughter to check up on her now?"

"You never just call to check."

"Well, I dare say..."

"I'm going to hang up now, if there's nothing else," Kelly snapped, already pulling the phone away from her ear.

"Okay, okay. I just wanted to know if you're going to be back," her mother said, all too patiently.

"Back?"

"For Canada Day, of course," her mother complained. "You already missed last year, you know."

"I told you, I had overtime work at that warehouse..."

"Right, I can't believe you worked there. Inhumane conditions, the papers say. What you were thinking, I don't understand... Can't you get a proper job?"

"Mom, I really need to go. Really," Kelly replied. "I'll... text you later, okay? With my answer."

"Text, I just don't get—"

Kelly's finger pressed down hard on the disconnect button, and stabbed at it again just in case before turning the ringer off and dropping the phone beside her laptop. It buzzed, but was ignored till it stopped. Only then did her shoulders release. She hated it, but she still felt trapped. By her life, by her career sometimes, by her parents and their expectations.

For a long time, she stared into space. Her thoughts swirled. Memories of paternal disappointment, degrees given up, and the sheer uselessness of it all. Of getting a little ahead, only for her car to break down and need repairs, or for her cat to need to see a vet. Going back and forth, never managing to make it anywhere.

Eventually she shook herself free of her stupor and returned to posting the menu and indulging in a trawl through that most medicinal of balms – cute cat videos.

More Prep and a Working Lunch

M o Meng listened to the girl and her mother as he worked, hands flying across the chopping board as he finished the first batch of pineapple cakes. With them in the oven and a timer set to let him know when it was time to extract them, he needed to get a move on the meal for tonight.

In this case, with such fresh produce in reach, it would be a shame to not make full use of it. First, he moved the collected liquid from the pineapple discards into a simple plastic tub before juicing a dozen more pineapples to get a sufficient quantity. A quick taste and a handful of brown sugar was added to help caramelization later. Of course, that was not all; generous additions of fresh, chopped ginger and garlic, a dollop of sesame oil, a dash of rice vinegar and some green onion finished off the marinade.

A quick step over to the fridge, and he pulled out the thawed slabs of flank-cut beef ribs he had set aside the day before. In this case, he had it pre-cut for him by a trustworthy orc butcher who had fallen into the trade just over three decades ago, trading broadsword for butcher's knife.

The extra-thin-cut ribs were perfect for the dish since they'd easily soak up the marinade. He put them into the plastic tubs to soak for the next few hours. Ensuring the containers were covered and the ribs fully submerged, he repeated the process till he had a couple of tubs prepped for the night.

By the time he was done, it was time to swap out one set of cake pans for another. The baked cakes were set aside to cool for a few minutes before Mo Meng would extract each cake by flipping it over. Then they'd go into the storage pantries, where simple runes helped keep the meal warm without drying the cakes out.

A little cheat, but in this case an acceptable one, he felt. After all, he had done the cooking by hand. It was just to keep the food at the optimal temperature that he was using magic now. Even if modern technology had come far, preservation runes still were well ahead of the game.

At least for now.

The first meat of the night was marinating, at least for one of the main courses. But you couldn't just prep for a single dish, not if you were running a restaurant. At least a few were required, never mind the vegetables and starches to go with it. Of course, you could do something like pasta, mix it all in, but since the theme of the night was barbecue, that wouldn't work.

No. He had his work cut out for him.

Mo Meng moved on to shucking corn. Sitting over a big trash bin, he worked quickly, stripping leaves and checking over the carb that had arrived earlier in the day. That was the thing that many did not realize about dining establishments and cooking for hundreds.

The days started early, ran late.

It was one reason he only had a single meal service. If he ran both lunch and dinner, he would be doing more work than he'd ever want. After all, while he enjoyed cooking, this was retirement – not an actual job.

As he prepped the kitchen for the upcoming service, he let his aura and senses expand, touching upon the formations all around him. He traced them with a mental hand, feeling for the worn-down patches as Mana coursed through them, the very fabric of magic wearing away the runes. Like an acid passing over metal, or water over stone, it eventually wore even the sturdiest down.

Not that he'd used the best for the restaurant. For one thing, he had not expected to stay so long. The business had been opened on a whim, put together over the course of a week with the aid of a little magic and a lot of favors. The level of industry that dwarves and gnomes and pixies could bring forth when properly motivated put most beings to shame.

It also helped, of course, that work ordinances were not something he bothered with. Simple 'stay away' runes kept pesky creatures like safety inspectors and fire marshals away. Any problem great enough that his magic could not handle it was not going to be fixed by having an extra physical exit or a sloping entrance for accessibility.

In the end, he'd never planned to be here this long. But the world changed and so had he. Finding a routine and joy in simple acts kept things interesting, and the runes would have lasted another century or so with the then-present level of environmental Mana.

Except for her return.

And the return of all the others.

"Boss?" Kelly's voice, interrupting his thoughts.

Looking up from where he was slicing the vegetables to prep a coleslaw accompaniment, Mo Meng raised an eyebrow at the interruption. Unusual, for her to bother him while he worked. Not that his hands ever stopped moving.

"Just wondering, did you want anything for lunch?"

"Lunch?" he said.

"Yeah. That meal in the middle of the day."

The look he gave her made her return a sickeningly sweet smile.

"You know, I'm standing in a kitchen."

"Of course. But I didn't want to presume," she said. "Also, I heard that cooks often get tired of cooking because, well…"

"We're always cooking for everyone else?" Mo Meng said, then inclined his head. "It was like that, when the cooking mattered. In the armies on the march, on the road…" He shook his head. "Even sometimes now, I'll admit, I have days when I choose not to cook. I have places I frequent."

"Oh?" Now she looked interested. "Any place I should look out for?"

"You'd trust my taste?"

Now it was her turn to return the look, before he chuckled. "A few local spots. Most are a little more…"

"International?" she said, shaking her head. "You've gotten more brazen lately. Ever since, well... she came."

"Lily." He hesitated then, thinking over his actions, the conclusions he'd reached without ever truly considering them. "It's important."

"What is?"

"Getting you ready," Mo Meng said. Seeing her mounting frustration, he gestured upwards to where the runes lay, carved into the ceiling beams and the pillars of the restaurant. "Things are changing."

Kelly stared at his face, searching it for clues. "You don't mean just the restaurant, do you?"

"No."

"I got that she's a big deal, but that big...?"

"It's not just her." He frowned. "Others are waking, because she is. Some, she's waking on purpose. Like a stone, striking others as it rolls down the mountain." He shook his head. "She's quite a big boulder. No little pebble. Some of the others wouldn't move for anyone but her."

"Are things going to get... dangerous?"

Mo Meng shook his head. "Most of the old ones went to sleep because they were tired of the fights. Tired of trying to change one another, change humanity. Though some might be a little angry at what has happened."

"To the world?"

"And the people they once cared for."

Kelly looked scared for a second, before he waved his hand. "It's fine. Humanity has learned too. And there are many who would stop them, if they chose to be obstinate." He chuckled. "It might take some a bit of time to realise how global the world is, but this interconnectedness, the understanding we've gained... it cuts both ways."

"I don't understand."

"It's hard to commit some of the more..." He paused, then shrugged. "...horrific actions without someone else taking offense. You can't exactly blow up a volcano anymore, not without everyone else getting angry at the soot and the mini ice age you've caused."

"That's a very specific example."

Mo Meng smiled, then finished pushing the lettuce and cabbage he'd been chopping aside, tossing it into the big container he had been using.

"Lunch?"

Kelly snorted. "I can see what you're doing, you know." When he offered her no answer, she sighed. "Lunch."

"Fried rice?"

"Again?" she complained.

"Fine." He chuckled, wandering over to the pantry. He peered inside for a bit before coming back, a loaf of fresh bread in hand. "Something different, then. But comfort food, right?"

"Uhh.... Yeah."

"Good."

A tap on the flat grill had it heating up. Bread met bread knife, inch-thick slices cut off within moments. The wheat bread was buttered, a generous dollop added on both sides of the thick slices. He placed the four pieces aside as the grill continued to heat while he wandered back to his fridge, searching inside for the remaining ingredients.

Bechamel sauce. Cheese, three types. Black Forest ham. He took those back to his table, slicing the ham into thin slices with a paring knife with quick swift motions. Next, he grated the cheeses, mixing them with a touch of the bechamel sauce to make sure the mixture would hold together. Once that was ready, he took the slices of bread and covered the inside with the bechamel sauce.

Back to the grill now, with all the ingredients in hand, carefully placing them in easy reach. A quick test with a drop of water showed it was heated enough as the water danced across the grill, before butter was added to grease the top. He waited a moment for the butter to melt before he placed the first slices on the grill, buttered sides down.

Swift movements layered the cheese slices on top of the bread, for they needed time to melt. One, two, three slices of gruyère, gouda and cheddar on the bread. A tap against the grill lowered the temperature a little, to give the cheese more time to melt before a dash of Dijon mustard was added to the top. Not direct to the bechamel sauce, or the bread, because that would muddy the taste. Then, slices of ham layered over the mustard, and then more cheese slices, even as the smell of the toasting bread began to waft upwards.

He breathed in, a small smile crossing his lips. Toasted bread, butter and bechamel sauce mixed with cheese. Another slice of bread on top of the mixed layers, the bechamel side down so that the buttered side was on top. He gently pressed on the bread, making sure the entire concoction was pushed tightly together, the entire sandwich flattened to ensure it would heat faster.

Occasionally he moved the bread around the grill, ensuring it did not stick, keeping an eye on it, but waiting.

That was the thing about cooking – so much of it was waiting. Waiting until the right moment when everything was ready, waiting for spices to mix, for herbs to soak in. Of course, once it was ready, you had to move fast.

More butter, then once it was melted, time to flip the sandwiches to warm the other side and crisp the bread and bechamel mixture. He rotated each sandwich, making sure it didn't stick, waited for the cheese and bechamel to warm and crisp up, wait for a couple of minutes till the cheese was melted and the ham was warmed. Next up, a metal cover over the top of the sandwiches, trapping the heat to speed up the melting of the cheeses.

"Grilled ham and cheese?" Kelly said, a small smile on her lips. "Very comforting."

"It should be. But no, not grilled ham and cheese sandwiches," Mo Meng said.

"Then what?"

No answer for the moment, as Mo Meng checked the ingredients on hand and made a face. Another journey to the refrigerator where he extracted some shredded parmesan cheese, and then he was back, waiting.

A check under the cover, letting out some moisture to allow the sandwiches to crisp rather than grow soggy. Checked each sandwich, making sure it was still able to move freely on the grill, verified that the cheese was melting. The blended cheeses were dripping down the sides a little, gooey and barely held together.

He pulled them both off the grill, turning it off as he left it, and placed them on a cookie tray with parchment paper to catch the cheese. Then, more bechamel sauce before the last of the cheese mixture with the grated parmesan was added on top of it all.

"What's that weird white stuff?"

"Bechamel sauce. Milk, cream, roux. Nutmeg and pepper. Traditional white sauce from France," Mo Meng said. "Necessary for the Croque Monsieur."

"Huh. Guess that's why this isn't a grilled cheese sandwich..." She eyed the messy concoction on top of the bread, even as she watched him slide the tray into the oven. "Uhh... how long is this going to take?"

"As long as it needs," Mo Meng said, chuckling. "About twenty more minutes."

"But it was ready!"

"It was grilled cheese ready," he said, as he stepped away from the oven to return his ingredients to their resting places and clean his grill. She watched him for a few moments, pouting a little as her stomach rumbled at the smell of melting cheese and fresh, toasted bread.

"You know, the way you said that makes me think there's a *but* in there..."

"Nothing wrong with grilled cheese sandwiches However, it isn't what I'm cooking."

"Also, isn't that a little sexist? Croque Monsieur? Mister Crock?"

"The 'croque' means crispy. Mister Crispy. There's a Madame Crispy too, if you wish."

Eyes narrowed as she wondered if he was teasing her. "What's that include?"

"A fried egg."

Silence greeted his words, as Kelly tried to decide if he was pulling her leg. When he glanced her way, having returned to his preparations, he noted her expression.

"I didn't name it."

"Fried eggs for women..." She rolled her eyes, then sighed. "Whatever. The French already gender everything anyway."

Smiling a little, Mo Meng kept an eye on the time as he worked, cleaning his hands a few minutes before time and flipping the oven to broil setting. He popped the oven open just a bit to eye the concoction, noting how everything was bubbling. The top had yet to achieve that burnt-golden colour that was necessary for a proper Croque Monsieur. Not a problem. That was the entire purpose of grilling it.

This was the tricky part, which was why he was taking his time to watch. Leave the cheese and sandwich in too long, and golden brown became brown, and then black and charcoal. It didn't take much, going from perfectly cooked and crispy and yellow to a burnt mess that had to be scraped away.

The moment it was ready, he pulled the tray out, an oven towel protecting his hand. Onto the tray top and then, set aside on a cutting board. Slice diagonally to make it easier to eat, then plated one on top of the other with the second slice placed at an angle. A touch of garnish on top to give it a burst of colour, a dash of plum sauce on the side if she wanted a taste of sweetness to add to the dish.

And it was done.

Croque Monsieur and Passing Afternoons

T he Croque Monsieur preceded its arrival with an olfactory assault. Crispy cheese, parmesan and warmed bechamel sauce with fresh, toasted bread beneath. The sharpness of toasted parmesan and the softer, more delicate aroma of the gruyere, gouda and cheddar combination beneath. Immediately her mouth watered, and Kelly straightened her spine as the meal arrived. She reached for the toast before frowning, realizing that there was no way to eat this without dirtying her hands.

"You know where the forks and knives are," Mo Meng said, reading her look of consternation with ease.

"One point for plain ham and cheese sandwiches, then," Kelly said with a sniff.

He snorted, watching as she retrieved the utensils and napkins, offering him his set. However, rather than dig in directly, he waited for her to do so. Used to this by now – there was, she assumed, no better sight for a chef than a person enjoying their cooking – she set to it.

The fork went down first, cracking the crispy and crunchy outer surface of the parmesan cheese on the bread, golden yellow and brown in turn. She pushed with her knife to slice off a corner of the triangle, feeling the utensil cut through the crisp bread and then the gooey cheese center. A single long stroke and a pull had the bread coming apart, though long strings of cheese, melted and glistening with oils, trailed after the bread as she raised her portion.

"Oooh…" She breathed out at the sight. Hidden among the cheese, the slices of light brown ham glistened, making her slaver just a little at the sight. She popped the entire thing into her mouth and began to chew, feeling the crunch of the toasted cheese and the crispiness of the bread first, the slight rubberiness of melted cheese and the heat of the just-baked meal filling her mouth.

"Hot, hot, hot!" she mouthed around the piece of bread, blowing hard through her open mouth to cool it. Even so, saliva flooded her mouth as the tartness of the parmesan combined with the silken feel of the gruyère and the hard crunch and crispness of the bread beneath.

The moment the piece cooled enough, she began chewing, swallowing the piece down and repeating the entire act on the next piece. The Croque Monsieur reminded Kelly of the best ham and cheese sandwiches, a mixture of sharp and rich cheeses combining with the saltiness of the ham in her mouth, all contrasting with the crispy bread. However, the bechamel sauce helped to smooth out the tartness and richness of the cheese, to make the ham less salty and the bread a tad less crispy.

In essence, then, the Croque Monsieur was a heavier, creamier version of a good grilled cheese sandwich, adding layers of subtle taste that a plain sandwich would lack.

Chewing and swallowing, she was done with one half before she knew it, her knife scraping against the plate as she tried to cut a non-existent portion off. She blinked, pushed against the random stupor that filled her and looked up to praise her boss. Only to be visited by a terrible new sight.

Mo Meng stood there, having forgone the use of utensils and just gripped the oily sandwich with one hand, chewing on his meal directly.

"Could use a little sweetness, I think," Kelly said, challengingly. Mostly because she could, rather than because she thought the meal required anything. "Maybe some apples?"

"Granny Smith, perhaps?" Mo Meng said, eyes glinting with amusement.

"I'm sure you've got some heirloom apple that's better, right?"

"As though I have connections for every kind of plant, animal and vegetable."

"That's not a no."

A grin was her only answer. He opened his mouth and slipped in the last morsel of sandwich before wiping his hands on a nearby napkin.

"So. Better or worse?"

"Mpphfff!" was her answer, to begin with. He waited until she had swallowed. "What is it that you always say? It's not a contest between dishes but what suits your mood at the time?"

"At the diner's time, yes." Mo Meng smiled. "Because food isn't just a matter of putting together a combination of high-quality ingredients and impeccable techniques. Cooking, and the meal itself, is just as much about the diner, the experience that they bring with them and their expectations.

"A location, its ambience, the plating and the servers, the company that one keeps ... it can all dictate how a meal can taste. It's why a dish from the past, cooked with love and care and warmth, can surpass even the most impeccable gourmet meal. A quickly cooked bowl of instant noodles at the top of a mountain after a day's hike can taste heavenly, a rival for any dish I could make.

"The people and circumstances of a meal matter."

"I like that." She smiled as he wound down, her head propped on her hand. "When you wax poetic about cooking."

Mo Meng inclined his head a little in acknowledgment. He picked up her empty plate, and took it with him back into the kitchen and the dishwasher. After all, he had hands to clean and more prep to complete.

In the meantime, wiping her own hands on a napkin, Kelly wandered back to her table and the laptop that awaited her attention.

A meal, with the right company and time, made all the difference. Perhaps that was why she kept coming back here, even though the number of problematical customers kept increasing and the workload kept piling on.

Gone was her sleepy job and the half-dozen customers a night she had been used to.

Gone was the chance to review her studies in-between serving occasional dishes.

Gone, but not forgotten, but the friends were still there.

It was hard to tell when day darkened to night, with the dim lighting offered by the half-sized basement windows set at ceiling height. The constant glow of electric lighting kept the restaurant well lit all through the day, and only the shifting shadow of windowsills as the sun trekked its way across the sky gave any indication of the environment outside.

In the kitchen, the constant clatter of preparation continued through the afternoon. Ingredients were chopped, eggs were cracked, fruit and potatoes peeled. At times, the sound of boiling water and grinding machines rose from within, even as the clatter of pots and pans echoed through the restaurant. Over the soothing sounds of industrious work, Kelly had hooked into the sound system, piping in a folky-pop Canadian singer. A deep, surprisingly husky voice echoed on, singing about digging up dinosaurs and pumping them through cars, crying about a past burned up for a future uncertain.

Head bent, she pecked away at the essay due for her college course. Sometimes she wondered why she continued to bother, but distance learning and a decreased course load – and the consequent lower cost – kept her industrious. Along with the inertia of expectations -- her own and those of the world outside.

Sucking on her lower lip in thought, she barely noticed the passing time, her crouched presence only occasionally broken by a trip to the washroom or a refill of her sarsaparilla cup, piped in from a keg – an actual keg that she had to exchange every week – near the bar. Those were the worst days, when she had to clean the tubes and the soda-machine contraption.

And all the while, words were placed, arguments with parental figures and looming rent bills forgotten as she broke down the first three Evil Dead movies and the remake for her professor, comparing and contrasting themes, videography and special effects for points on an essay that might barely be read.

Time passed and eventually her alarm went off. Books and laptop were stored in her backpack, the pack secreted in the small employee closet just behind the stairs. An apron was taken, donned over her clothing, and order pads and pens added. Finally, shoes were switched out from fashionable streetwear to comfortable and practical sneakers that were almost magical in their ability to keep her feet and lower back from aching.

Well, perhaps not *almost* magical. She was quite certain that Mo Meng had a deal with a brownie family or two, who took care of the routine maintenance tasks required in a big restaurant like this. Certainly, after the first day when she'd left the shoes behind rather than take them home, they'd not only fit better but were more comfortable than ever.

Sadly, it seemed that they only did their work on work-related items. The torn handbag and the broken heel of her third favorite pair of high heels had never been fixed.

A girl had to try.

Work clothes in place and hair pinned up, Kelly started her own prep. Chairs had to be lowered, tables wiped down, the floor swept once again. Not that the restaurant was ever dirty, but it was old and the bricks and ceiling joists above had a tendency to shed dust and the occasional flake of paint.

Sometimes she wondered about Mo Meng. He could have magicked it all away, she was certain. No matter what that new mage said, that Henry, surely someone as old as Mo Meng had the skills to take care of such mundane things.

Then again, Mo Meng might have used magic in the days before she was hired. Or perhaps not; she could imagine him slowly sweeping away, wiping tables down by himself. Content in the rote work of maintenance, taking comfort in the routine.

It was hard to tell sometimes, his temperament and views on the matter seeming to shift like the wind or the tides. Altering at a whim, as events and people arrived.

Still, as much as she might dislike wiping things down, he didn't wield magic on such mundane tasks. For one thing, it would mean fewer hours for her. For the other, the routine tasks were grounding, comforting in the way they were similar to other jobs she'd had.

A way to transition from the world outside to the one within, a world of magic and unique customers.

A New Customer

The thing about magic was that it was always around. Like gravity in a midnight-lit cave, light waves on a sunny day or the electrical impulses within a mind, it existed without one necessarily noticing. All it required to use magic was the ability, the willingness and the knowledge to reach out and nudge it.

That was, of course, the problem with magic, too. You couldn't exactly regulate air. You couldn't put a price on it, or stop someone else from consuming it. Obviously, you could capture it, compress it, maybe feed it to some foolish rich person or short-breathed hospitalized patient for more money.

For the supernatural, the very existence of magic, and their ability to wield it, was just a part of their existence. Inherent glamours in elves, the ability to shift between dimensions for ghosts, the formation of ectoplasmic goo for pengalang. Attempting to control their access was impossible.

Which was why the Department of Supernatural Entities had been formed.

Their goal was not to regulate magic. It was not even to regulate the existence of sometimes dangerous, multitudinous and often chaotic species that wielded magic in all its forms. Instead, their goal was to track, record, educate and mitigate those existences as they went about their daily lives, bumping into and interacting with the mass of humanity that had neither the desire nor the wherewithal to handle the existence of the supernatural.

Nor the need, if Agents of DESE had anything to say about it.

Which, mostly, they did.

"So, why is this restaurant marked as 'Unnamed'?" A hand waved the big tablet-phone around. Unlike most sleek modern technology, this tablet-phone was in a wooden case, with crystals embedded at the four cardinal points. To the everyday eye, it just looked like a blinged-out phone case—an excuse that bubbly, pixie-cut brunette who was waving it about had used more than once. As for the magically-inclined, they might notice the Mana projectors embedded in it, allowing the tablet to showcase some of the more esoteric data that the agency stored. "Google has it as the Nameless Restaurant."

"Officially, there has not been a name given to the restaurant," the heavyset DESE agent that walked beside her, each of his steps worth twice hers, said with quiet patience. The pair were dressed in semi-formal business wear, which in both cases meant dark suits but no ties.

"What about for permits?" Ophelia – O to everyone who didn't want a cutting word – asked, nose wrinkling. "I've heard – from an ex – about how annoying all the paperwork the government throws at you is."

"Your boyfriend was right. That's partly why we're here. A fact you'd know if you read the brief," Mika Sacher said.

"Sorry, boss!" O chirped, ducking her head. "I thought background on the naga clans we were meeting was more important, you know. Their annual birthing cycle was always something we were warned to look out for in the academy, especially if it ran up against other supernatural mating cycles."

"It is. And the restaurant and its owner are usually a non-issue," Mika admitted.

"Usually?"

"Their wards are failing. Or being allowed to fail. Hard to say, with everything going on. Now, we've got more humans coming in, and more supernaturals and actual bureaucrats asking about them. It was one thing when they were discreet about it, but we've got to head it off before it creates even more paperwork."

"Right. So what's the game plan?"

"Softly, softly of course. You read his file."

"Of course!" O said. "But just in case I didn't..."

"The principal is an uncategorized, non-aligned Mage. From secondary sources, we know he predates the Mage Council and is thus grandfathered into his status under the Merlin protocols."

"I hate those."

"Doesn't everyone?" Mika said, wryly. "But better that than, well...."

"Trying to enforce laws that we have no way of making stick?" She shook her head. "How is it that all these old fellas have teleportation and haven't just, you know, revolutionized transportation?"

"Because until recently, with the advent of GPS and modern astronomy, the actual act of teleportation was... tricky. Miss a few decimals when transporting yourself across the planet and you're not showing up outside of a field, you're *inside* the field. Also the energetic levels required to transport matter over a large area could only be managed by those at the highest levels." Mika shook his head. "We're off-topic, though."

"Right! Uncategorized, ancient Mage with unknown but extremely powerful magic and magical knowledge." She nodded. "Anything else?"

"The regulars. Other supernaturals, of course, and one normal."

"A norm?" O repeated, surprised.

"Yes. All indications are that she's in the know, but mundane."

"Unable or unwilling?"

"To gain magic?" Mika shrugged, their footsteps finally having taken them most of the way to the doorway. Inset in a side alleyway, hidden between a couple of dumpsters and out of plain sight, most would have walked right by it. No sign, no indicator hung above or on the doorway to indicate the presence of a restaurant. Some might have called it a speakeasy, but while alcohol was served there, it was by far not the focus.

At least, that was what Mika had been told by the previous case worker. He'd been rather put-off by the fact that he had been transferred, but that was part and parcel of the job. Too many supernaturals had ways of gaining control over DESE personnel, subtly or unconsciously. Thus, regulations required the regular rotation of personnel between cases and individuals.

"Gotcha. Listen and learn, and then broach the subject of licensing and paperwork later," O said, firmly.

"Or set up an appointment for that, later."

O bobbed her head in acknowledgment of her mistake. She glanced to the side, seeing Mika hesitate at the door. He ran a hand down his suit, touched the cuff links, the silver bracelet and belt buckle he wore. She blinked and tapped her own enchantments, checking them over before giving him a sharp nod.

Hand on door handle, he pushed it open.

Making Entrances

“ **S** orry! Sorry. We’re not open just yet!”

Kelly hurried over, waving her hands over her head in a futile attempt to stop the pair from seeing inside. The doorway led to a concrete landing with a metal banister, just large enough for two people to stand on, that turned at a right angle and descended via a concrete staircase to the floor of the restaurant. It also, coincidentally, gave said newcomers an impressive view of the surroundings as they entered. A view which right now consisted of a lot of empty tables.

“Our apologies. The listing said it opened at five p.m.?” The speaker was a large man with a sharp, angular nose and a knowing look in his eyes. He wore a severe business suit, charcoal gray set-off by a pink shirt beneath.

His companion's gray suit and olive-green blouse were more stylish, better cut than the man's off-the-rack edition. As she stepped past the bulk of her friend to the railing, her eyes twinkled with curiosity and good humor, though there was something in the way she looked – more up towards the runes than down at her and the tables – that twigged Kelly's intuition.

Not that it mattered, so long as they were just customers. "I keep changing that, and someone keeps 'correcting' the listing to say five." She shook her head. "I swear, there's got to be a gremlin at work."

"Maybe." A flicker of looks between the two, while they hovered uncertainly on the landing. "Should we…?"

"Let them in," Mo Meng's voice cut through the noise, managing to make its way from the kitchen to them without being distorted. "They can hear the menu and have some water while we finish preparations."

Kelly began to turn towards the kitchen before stopping herself, plastering a customer service smile on her face. "Of course. Come in, come in. How about this one?" she said, waving to a table close to the entrance.

"Well, I was hoping to perhaps sit a little further in?" the bigger man said, offering a smile. "I'm Mika, by the way."

"Oh! Right. Sorry. Kelly. I'll be your server and host today. And that's Mo Meng, the owner, in the kitchen. He mostly cooks." A sharp glance within. "And leaves me to take care of the front of the house."

"Yes, of course," Mika murmured.

"I'm so sorry. And you can call me O, K!" Grinning at her little joke, O flounced right past Kelly to grab a seat closer to the kitchen, staring through the open pass at the figure within. She flopped into her chair with a little sigh, almost sprawling in it. Mika followed along more sedately while Kelly whisked a pair of glasses filled with cold water over to them.

"No ice?" O said, surprised.

"No. The owner doesn't believe in it," Kelly said. "We chill the glasses and the water so that it's cold, but not freezing. Try it!"

Raising an eyebrow, O took a sip and then blinked. She took another sip, frowning as she raised the glass and stared at the contents.

"This isn't tap water," she said slowly. Beside her, Mika repeated her actions, pausing too to shoot Kelly an inquiring look.

"Well, it is. But we've got a special filtration system to help remove some of the impurities and other chemicals. Makes it taste a lot better, and it'd be a waste to put ice in it, afterwards."

"Could just freeze the water," O offered.

Kelly could only offer a smile to that comment before she continued. "Would you like to know about our menu for today?"

"I'd like to see it," O said.

Now Mika let out a huff, nudging her with his shoe under the table. O ignored it, watching as Kelly shook her head, answering with rote but pleasant words.

"We don't have one. The restaurant alters its menu daily, so we choose not to waste paper. It's also not very diverse, though I can guarantee you that it's all very tasty."

"Oh?"

"Yes. Would you like me to list it out now?" Kelly said.

"Why don't you just bring us whatever you think is best," O said with a smile, eyes glinting with mischief.

Mika frowned at O before he added to Kelly. "Anything that is kosher, if you will."

"Of course. I'll let the chef know."

When Kelly had drifted off, he glared at O. "Don't order for me."

"Sorry. She just annoys me." A single raised eyebrow met her statement. "No, I don't know why. It's just something about her…"

"Professional. That's what we endeavor to be. Please remember. Being new is only an excuse for a little while," Mika said, firmly.

"Eh, she's just a mundane…" But when he continued to glare, she dipped her head. "I'll be good."

"Very well."

Having passed on the order for Mo Meng to handle when he was ready, Kelly returned to the prep required to set up the restaurant. The cash register was powered on, the petty cash checked, the counters wiped down and extra water jugs extracted.

No coconut water today or any other special drinks, so it was just water for the most part. Mo Meng occasionally brought out special alcohols to go with certain meals, wines or other hard liquor, but it was not a regular occurrence. That being so, water would be the main liquid refreshment for the evening, which meant that Kelly had to ensure that the filter was running at full capacity and as many jugs were pre-extracted as possible.

In the meantime, the pair of agents took in the restaurant. Mika extended his senses carefully, testing the edges of the wards, surreptitiously reading the ones high above him. Not that it mattered, given the frank regard with which O surveyed the surroundings, getting up at one point to wander to the back of the building where a hallway led to the washrooms.

It was there, her head poked into a closet filled with janitorial equipment and other consumables, that Kelly found her. Arms crossed, the waitress cleared her throat, waited a moment, did it again, and when O continued to ignore her, gave the door a slight kick to let it bang against the woman's shoulder.

"What was that for?" O snapped, pulling her head out.

"Ooops. My foot must have slipped," Kelly said, sweetly. "But you won't find the washroom in there."

"I know."

"Good, then you can close the door and go to the washroom or return to your seat."

"And what if I said no?"

"Then I'd ask you to leave."

"And then?" O smirked, crossing her arms over her suit.

Kelly looked her up and down, then smiled broadly. "Well, I'm sure I'd figure something out."

"I think I'd like to see you try." Squaring her feet, O moved her hands from her sides, only to jump when a throat was cleared right behind her ear. Scowling, she spun about to find Mo Meng staring down at her with those placid black eyes. No threat was spoken as he regarded her.

"Right. Washroom?" O said, trying to contain the sudden nervousness she felt. Not that recrossing her arms over her chest and hunching down hid it.

"Down the hall," Kelly said, watching as the woman scurried to the washroom. She followed the woman long enough to see her enter before she turned to Mo Meng, only to find him gone already. Letting out a little huff, the waitress closed the closet door.

Later.

She'd deal with overly inquisitive customers later.

The Grill

In the kitchen, Mo Meng continued to work, allowing his clone to disperse and the hair he had used to make it fall to the ground. The Ten Thousand Transformations technique was quite useful, though rather energy-intensive, which was why he preferred not to use it anywhere but inside his place of power. It was also rather unhygienic in the kitchen. Shedding hairs around his foodstuffs was just bad form, never mind the fact that he was working for fun.

Part of the key to happiness was learning to enjoy the work one did, no matter how simple or dull it might seem. The pleasure of doing a job well was a goal every individual could pursue, if they wished to.

Agents were always a bother, especially new ones. They hadn't learned to enjoy the process. Over the years, it seemed that most fell into a few major categories. Angry and jealous was only one. Those like O so badly wanted to be a mage, to be special, to be chosen somehow and thus become part of the supernatural world. To be more. Yet, because of circumstances or training or just biology, they could never manage it.

Some eventually learned to live with it, accepting their role as overseers and bureaucrats of the supernatural. Others moved on, finding peace in staying far away from the supernatural. And a few, a rare few, took the plunge; doing whatever it took to acquire that spark of magic or obsession that made them feel left out.

It mattered little, beyond the need to keep an extra eye on her. As for her ostensible senior agent and boss, he was playing oblivious and sipping his drink. The minor shifts in his aura were more than enough to reveal his irritation with his partner, though, and Mo Meng assumed a much longer, quieter discussion would take place. Later, of course.

For now, Mo Meng was working on the next category item of his menu, which were the side dishes. Right now, a series of deep pots of well-salted water were roiling, whole washed yellow potatoes within boiling. A small timer stood nearby, ticking off how much longer he needed to keep them in.

With such a rich meal, heavy with sugar and vinegar, Mo Meng intended it to be accompanied by a blander side dish that could soak up the taste and complement the main rather than contrast with it. The simplest option would have been a big plate of white rice. Maybe top it off with a touch of butter, if you wanted to give it some additional creaminess. Risotto was another option, though that would make the meal significantly heavier, the starchiness of the rice variant too heavy as anything but the main.

Simple, but he was going with a theme here. While sweet potatoes – or yams – would suit the flavor profile, he had a large number of extra potatoes on hand and none of the others. Best not to waste, and so Mo Meng was leaning toward the classic for the sides.

Potatoes – cut rustic style to give a little texture to the potatoes and a bit more of a homey nature to the dish – in the pot. Let them boil, while he started the grill and heated it. He wanted the grill hot before he started placing his other side dish – corn – on it. Of course, the un-shucked corn was soaking in a tub of water, pressed down with another pot, so that the leaves would be properly damp. Leaving the leaves on and wet helped keep the corn from burning on the grill and steamed it in its own flesh, leaving it moist rather than overly dry.

All the while, as he moved between stations, cleaning, wiping down, and checking on his dishes, the constant hum of industrial fans and boiling water filled the air, the scent of the baking pineapple upside down cakes lingering, mixing with the boiling water and potatoes, the charcoal in the grill and the wood chips.

Outside the kitchen, voices, the quiet discussion of the two agents as one was taken to task. In the meantime, Kelly cleaned the tables, set down chairs and wrapped utensils, prepping for the flood of customers that had become their norm.

Busy, busy, busy.

Mo Meng checked the heat over the grill, decided to hurry things along and began the process of moving some of the corn over. He put it on the unheated side for now, letting it warm up via indirect heat.

The fire was fueled by gas, but a bed of coals lay beneath the burners, glowing and ashing a little to provide a more consistent, wider warmth. So long as he took care to shift some of the cooler coals underneath the newly placed corn, he could keep the overall heat in that portion of the grill quite high while leaving himself the option of adjusting the temperature more carefully over the burners.

Tricky, managing such a complicated barbecue grill. Made more difficult by the shifting heat of the coals. It was why he had multiple thermometers placed along the edges of the grill, giving him an idea of the temperature at each point. While he had learned most of his craft without such tools, there was no point in being stubborn and eschewing modern conveniences.

Scattered under the charcoal were wood chips, applewood and oak. Not too much, just enough to give the whole grill a tantalizing smell. A simple push at the wards kept the smell contained to the grill itself and out the front of the kitchen, tempting those seated within without affecting the rest of his ingredients.

Corn placed, on the unheated side, enough that he could begin.

Next up, the meat on the hotter side of the grill. He needed to get it down now for it to cook properly. Needed to move some of the corn higher too, eventually, or else he wouldn't have enough space. Juggling act, but he had around ten minutes, while the skin crisped.

Meat down, the smell of fat and skin crisping in the air.

Now Mo Meng moved on to the pots of boiling water. He hummed to himself as he worked, dumping water out into the kitchen with care, huge clouds of steam rising to surround him as he worked. He kept his eyes slitted and his body leaning back a little as he waited for the steam to clear, making sure not to lose any of the precious potatoes.

Once done, he lowered the heat on the same burner and put the potatoes sans water back on the stove, leaving them to dry out. It would be easy to mash the potatoes immediately after draining, but giving the spuds a few more minutes to dry ensured that the resulting potatoes were creamy, not waterlogged and gummy-tasting.

It also bought him time, for he had another pot to deal with.

Mashing potatoes used to be a pain and a half, but once again, modern conveniences saved the day. A blender with the right paddle attachment took over the job once the potatoes were ready, though not before the necessary ingredients were added.

What those were could start a fistfight or two in the South, and more than one family feud. Everyone had their own ratios, their own secret ingredients. Mo Meng was no different, but for this course, he went with something traditional. No paprika to add color and bite, no cheddar to suit American tastes or cauliflower to give it substance or bacon to add crunch and a savory edge.

Into the pot went whole sticks of butter, a small amount of pre-roasted garlic cloves and pre-heated heavy cream. Of course, salt and pepper, the chef testing as he watched the paddle turn. With each rotation, the mixture grew creamier and thicker, a trusty little spoon occasionally dipped into it. He knew when it was ready when it grew creamy and fluffy, when the specks of yellow from the roast garlic became part of the dish.

He pulled it away before the mixture became too gummy from being overworked, and he was on to the next pot. He knew he was likely making too much, but it was getting hard to gauge quantities, what with the restaurant's newfound popularity.

Anyway, there were a number of simple recipes one could make with leftover mashed potatoes, if one was creative. If nothing else, frying them with a mixture of bacon, cheese and more garlic made for some great potato cakes.

Though that was more a breakfast dish.

No use for the restaurant, but he knew a few food banks that could always use a hand.

Daydreaming about what to do with leftovers that might never appear, Mo Meng finished with the potatoes, moving the mixture into the pre-heated ovens to keep warm. Not for long, because dinner would come all too soon.

Not a moment too soon, as he skimmed back to the grill; checking on temperatures and shifting some of the coals. He started turning the corn over and shifted some of it higher, above the grill. Letting the heat continue to cook it, slow and steady. He'd finish it, shuck it later, when there was space. When the orders started coming in, to free up grill lines.

A glance at the time and Mo Meng frowned. He was running late. At this rate, he might not have time to do a proper job, at least not in the way he was envisioning, nor the rest of the meal for today. The meat would take a couple of hours.

Funny, how not cooking for large numbers for a few decades meant you lost your touch. Then again, cooking on the road for an army or a caravan was quite a different thing than putting together a proper meal in a restaurant. Experience and the type of experience mattered.

A slight grimace on his lips, Mo Meng mentally reviewed his menu, trying to decide what he could sacrifice, what he could change or alter. And not once did his hands stop, as they flew across the grill.

Unnatural Relations

E leanor was the first to arrive, the elegantly dressed lady swanning into the restaurant moments after Kelly unlocked the door. She smiled widely at the waitress, going so far as to lean in and give her a peck on the cheek as she slipped inside. If she took a little sniff as she finished the kiss, no one commented.

"Lovely pair of earrings, my dear." Eleanor reached out and tilted Kelly's chin with a practiced movement, two fingers gently pressuring the waitress so that she had no choice but to turn her head. "Heirloom?"

"No." Kelly stepped back, pulling herself away from the fingers. She touched the dangling precious stones and gold earrings, running a finger down them as she added. "Vintage, I think. Found them while thrifting."

"Oh, how quaint." Eleanor's eyes glittered.

"Love your hair," Kelly replied in turn, smiling a bit as she edged herself over to give Eleanor room to walk by.

"I do like the color. I always wanted to be a redhead," Eleanor said, smiling. It was a beautiful scarlet, shaded perfectly and with exquisite care, by a hairdresser that probably cost half as much as most people's rent. Even in Toronto. It set off the woman's pale skin amazingly, though she lacked the freckles to complete the look.

"I tried it once… so much upkeep," Kelly replied in turn with a small smile.

"True, but that's what servants are for, dear." With that, Eleanor stepped down the stairs, brushing past Kelly with a slight sway of her hips. High heels clacked on the concrete as she headed for her usual table. Then she paused, eyes widening a little as she caught sight of the other occupants. "Mika. My, what a pleasant surprise."

"Auntie Eleanor," Mika said, standing up and bowing to her a little. There was a strained smile on his lips as she came over, his gaze fixed on her face and not the generous amount of cleavage she was sporting in her pale blue evening gown, one more suited to a fashionable soirée than the Nameless Restaurant. "You are looking well."

"And yet, you're hardly looking."

"Auntie!" he said, voice half-strangled.

Her answering smile was bright and perhaps a tad cruel. Eleanor next turned her attention to O, who was staring at the pair, a frown marring her face. "And who's this? Your date?"

"No! My partner."

"Ooooh, that was fast. Did you tell your parents?"

"Not that kind!"

Piercing eyes roamed over O's disapproving face. "Good. You could do better."

"Miss Di Rossi, I am sure you understood what Agent Sacher meant," O said, firmly. "I am Agent Ophelia Eliades of the Department of Supernatural Entities."

"Ophelia..." Eleanor's eyes narrowed. O, to her credit, did not flinch as Eleanor leaned in, drew a deep breath and stared into O's eyes. Quizzical brown met jealous green before Eleanor rocked back on her heels. "Not a seer, then."

O frowned. "And how do you know that?" She cocked her head to the side. "Your file had no indication of significant magic ability."

"Files, paperwork." A deep sigh. "Live long enough and you know what signs to look for in a seer." Eleanor turned back to Mika, who had let out a slight, relieved beath as she pulled away from his partner. "So, Mika my dear, what are you doing here? On official business, no less."

Mika offered her an apologetic smile while answering, "Just going through my new case assignments." He nodded towards the kitchen in quiet indication of what he meant.

"Oh. How interesting." She turned, glanced at the table that Kelly was standing beside, a glass of water and utensils already placed. "I shall leave you to it, then. You and your *partner*."

Her last words elicited a small groan from Mika even as the older woman sauntered over to her seat and sat, crossing one leg over the other elegantly. She crossed her hands primly, moving the simple slip that hung over her shoulder to the chair beside her.

Kelly noted, however, how she listened rather than asked about the menu. Listened to the pair of agents speak, heads bent low and whispering. Even as the waitress moved to finish final preparations, she could not help but overhear the conversation as well.

"—mingling with supernaturals are prohibited."

"My association – my family's association – with Aunt Eleanor happened long before I joined the ranks of DESE. It's all well catalogued, reviewed and understood by our superiors," Mika said. "So you need not worry about any improprieties."

"I'll be the judge of that," O said.

"No, you won't." Lowering his voice, Mika leaned in. "I'm the supervisor here. Don't think I didn't notice the altercation. Our job is to observe, understand and then adjudicate. We do not antagonize. We do not enforce."

Lips pressed tight, O looked mulish and ready to argue further with Mika.

Kelly would have preferred to continue listening, but by that point, she'd noticed that Eleanor had settled, sipped at her cup of water once and was now looking at her. It was time to return.

"So, what does our chef have for us today?" The woman smiled widely, the glint of too-sharp canines flashing for a moment on marble-pale skin and cherry-red lips. Head tilted to the side, she watched the moving figure in the kitchen where he worked over the grill. "Something a little... meaty... I hope. His experiment with vegan cuisine was... not his best."

"It was actually quite popular with many of our other guests," Kelly corrected gently.

A sniff was all the answer she received in return.

"You'll be pleased to know that Chef Mo has prepared a menu more to your liking today. To begin with, we have Maui ribs soaked in a pineapple marinade with sides of corn…" Kelly rattled off the menu with ease, only having to glance down twice to read the notes she'd taken. Even if the menu changed every day, the number of dishes was never too large.

"Those ribs sound lovely," Eleanor said after Kelly had run down. She paused for a moment before adding. "And, of course, the dessert."

"Of course." A slight inclination of her head as Kelly jotted down the order. She headed for the kitchen, tearing the top slip off her order book.

Only to be surprised when she spotted Mo Meng at the pass-through. He was not watching her but the door, his brows furrowed. As she watched, he took the order slip straight from her hand as he muttered under his breath.

"Now, what is he doing here?"

"Who?"

"Guest."

He shook his head, stepping away to place the order on the carousel.

Leaving Kelly puzzled, frowning at the silent doorway.

Honey Soy Chicken Legs

Mo Meng felt him approaching, his presence like a high-pressure front rolling across his magical senses. A coming storm, full of noise and bluster, arriving too soon for all magical beings to fasten their windows and shut their gates.

He was not the only one to notice the incoming storm. Eleanor's head rose, a hand touching her glass of water as she ran a long tongue along red lips. She turned, stared at the sigils encompassing the room before she made herself relax.

Not long after, the doorway opened, and the short, rotund figure of Tobias arrived. He stomped in, giving a brusque nod to Kelly before taking a seat. She brought over his water, telling him the extent of the menu that had been prepared; but already jotting his order down. Tobias was as reliable as the mountains. One of everything.

When she was done, she made her way to the kitchen again. She stared at Mo Meng, a puzzled look on her face as she carried the order slip, unsure of his earlier words. He didn't say anything, of course. There wasn't anything to say.

Not yet.

Mo Meng took note, glanced at his sides and walked over to where he'd left the meat to rest in the marinade. It was a simple recipe, the sauce having been prepared the day before. The ingredients were a mixture of honey, ketchup, molasses, brown sugar, water, vinegar and soy sauce that had to be thickened by boiling. A generous handful of garlic powder, tablespoons of mustard and paprika rounded out the recipe, giving it a necessary touch of heat.

Letting it rest the day before allowed the spices to marry further. Much like a good curry or a burgeoning relationship, a good barbecue sauce needed time to settle. Rush the process and the results were fine, but subpar. Time, time, improved it all.

Adjusting the temperature of the grill, Mo Meng checked it over and everything on it. He moved the corn up, shucked a few more ears and moved them to the back of the grill where they could cook, and begin to get the necessary score lines. He'd have to flip them around soon.

The meat he'd placed earlier in the day was cooked, score lines highlighted on lighter skin. Now was the time to finish it off. That meant the barbecue marinade and a brush, rolling over the skin for the last few minutes. Not when it was cooking, because then all you would get was ash, but later, in the last twenty minutes, ten on each side.

The smell, sweet and salty, caramelized honey and ketchup, drifting upwards.

The chicken was all dark meat. While the recipe worked well with just drumsticks or thighs, it always felt lacking to serve either piece alone. No, keeping the entire leg together was the best way to do things, as far as he was concerned.

Better.

He kept a small portion of grill open, a section so that he could begin searing the next batch. Mo Meng used his tongs, picked up the next set of raw chicken legs to place on the grill. A quick brushing of oil on the skin side to ensure it would not stick. All the pieces had been salted and peppered, of course.

Placement on the grill was skin side down. He heard the hiss and sizzle, the spitting of the grill as the fatty skin made contact.

He worked, waited.

Best not to mess, because once placed, it was best to leave the pieces untouched until they were ready. Patience, because you needed to wait for the right moment. Wait, for basted barbecue chicken that was whole to cook. For the skin to crisp, so you could flip it over without making a mess. Without portions of chicken skin sticking, even with the oil in play.

Of course, just throwing on what you had was a recipe for flare-ups. Better to take the time, to prep the chicken beforehand. Trim excess fat and skin from the pieces, set it aside for later use. Of course, purchasing good quality chicken beforehand helped, creatures that weren't forced to live their lives in cages. That had a chance to move around, to exist before their eventual demise. It was good to avoid unnecessary cruelty, even if one only wanted better dishes.

Fill one side, the cooler side above the coals, with more chicken so that it could heat slowly. Keep the other pieces moving, basting them as you went along. The smell of crisping chicken skin wafting through the air, mixing with the barbecue sauce.

Work fast, work efficiently, keep an eye on the thermometers. If that was all he had to do, it'd be simple. It wasn't, of course. He had more.

In this case, the remaining sides.

Simple enough to extract the chilled coleslaw from the fridge. Having prepped the cabbage beforehand and added enough salt to let the moisture be drawn out and drip out before combining with the rest of the shredded vegetables, the coleslaw was a mixture of chopped green and red cabbage, carrots, turnip, green apples and Vidalia onions. After that, a mixture of mustard, buttermilk, milk and vinegar finished up the recipe, along with a generous helping of black pepper and salt.

Sweet coleslaw, thick and heavy mashed potatoes with a touch of garlic and a portion of cream and butter, and barbecued corn to round out the sides. Then it was just a question of which meat to add to the meal, whether the diners wanted the ribs or the chicken legs.

The ribs would cook fast, so he would start them later. No point in drying them out by grilling them too soon. Mo Meng also had to add in time to rest the chicken legs, time for the meat to cool, for the juices to stay where they should be.

Now, the only problem was the incoming guests and the orders already here.

He had no time. He was already by the grill, checking everything over, rotating pieces around. Testing to make sure the corn was cooking, that the score lines were turned.

He was running behind.

He needed a solution.

And still, the storm was coming.

A Breaded Shelter

Down the block. A man, head turning side-to-side. Pressure, atmospheric, magical. Wind rising and making passersby wish for their coats. A few, a lucky few, gripped their coats tighter. Fall, the calendar said, but it was a summer heat that baked the sidewalks. Not that everyone had paid attention, or planned for the heat before they left.

The man stopped, that wave front. He stared upwards at the trees lining the sidewalk. Some were young, some were scrawny, lacking the proper nutrition. Some leaves had changed color, some trees sported a few bare branches.

Energy unfurled, that pressure never lessening even as some of it escaped. It went deep, into the soil beneath the concrete pavements, into the water and nutrients beneath. The energy pulsed, flowed deep within.

Nothing drastic, nothing startling happened.

Not yet.

Mo Meng sensed it all, felt the energy unfurling blocks away. He ignored the energy playing out, focused instead on what he had to do. A solution to his problem.

A smile as he found one. One quick check, then he hurried off to the pantry. He should, if he was right, have the ingredients. A solution that resolved multiple problems at the same time, almost like magic.

The best kind, really.

He pulled the bread out, extracted the bread knife from its resting place and began slicing. Quick motions, parting the loaf. Hopefully, the couple of loaves he had left over would be enough.

Room-temperature butter, taken from its spot, was used to butter both sides. No space on the barbecue grill, so he turned on the toaster oven. He prepped the rack, dropping slices of buttered bread on it, his other hand working a semi-solid bar and pulling long slivers clear. Each sliver he dropped onto a tiny serving tray, for those who might want more butter on theirs.

Stop, long enough to check the barbecue.

Back to the toaster and the rack, which he slid under. As he waited for the bread to grill, he went back to working on the butter dishes and the accompanying sides. He couldn't just send out the bread and butter, not if he wanted to meet all his objectives.

As he worked, the presence he'd sensed finally made it to the street.

The front door of the Nameless Restaurant swung open, spilling fading sunlight into the room. The figure coming through had a young, fashionable haircut – shaved short on the sides, sweeping upwards in the front and a little long in the back. It was shot through with streaks of black, predominantly white otherwise. A simple, close-cropped Van Dyke beard outlined the seamed face, the prominent Anglo-Saxon nose jutting out.

Clothing followed; a hair metal band cover on a black t-shirt and faded blue jeans clothed the body, the addition of a short green cape the only particularly surprising item in the man's outfit. Well, that and the long walking stick he used.

The moment he entered, the entire room focused upon the man, drawn to his entrance like metal filings to a lodestone. There was unseen presence to him, an aura of power that was entirely visible on the other planes but was shrouded for those in the mundane world.

Which was, probably, why the pair of impatient young professionals standing right behind the newcomer growled.

"Well, move it, old man. We didn't come here early just to stand around!"

The quiet intake of breath was all the louder in the pin-drop silence of those within as they waited to see his reaction.

A New Guest and an Old Friend

The old man, the new guest, turned with the ponderous grace of a living mountain. Like watching a landslide begin and pick up speed, the very air hummed with the friction of his movement. Without thought, Kelly found herself moving, crossing the too-big – hah! she had never thought that before of the restaurant – space to avert disaster.

"Pardon me?" the old man whisper-said. Innocuous words, but filled with hidden threat.

"I..." A visible gulp, and then the younger man rallied. "I said, move." Then, as though prompted by an invisible guardian angel – or perhaps the sudden flinch and too-tight grip on his arm of his companion – he added. "Please?"

Silence greeted his request and the young man swayed on his feet. Taller than the old man, somehow it still seemed that he was being loomed over. His companion gripped his arm, fingers pale against the sleeve. They feared the old man now, struggled to speak or move—as though a hidden threat was upon them, even as the humming noise in the not-air was whispering warnings. A storm cloud of magical potential darkness, waiting to be unleashed.

From behind Kelly muttered curses erupted, while little devices clipped to the Agents' belts, devices that looked like pictures of old-school beepers, began to beep and jitter. A glance behind found new illumination highlighting the undersides of jaws and hands as green lights lit, one after the other.

Then she was on the staircase, first foot on the riser and looking up at the silent tableau.

"Welcome to the Nameless Restaurant, sir." Kelly clutched her notepad before her chest like a shield as she chirped the greeting. "Party of one?"

Tilting his head to the side, the old man looked down at Kelly. "Party of one? I am no Dionysus, or Sucellus, to do so."

"Just a saying," Kelly said. "Do you have a reservation?"

The older man shook his head. With each moment, that looming sense of disaster faded as his attention was refocused. Behind him, the pair of mundanes were silent, unwilling to move in case they attracted his wrath once more. "No. Is it required?"

"Not at all! We generally do not take reservations." Kelly stepped back and swept her hand down and out, gesturing now into the restaurant. "Should I take your... cape?" She stumbled over the last word.

"If it will let you." Descending, a little smile dancing on his lips, he turned to offer his back. Surprise registered on his face, quickly wiped away, as Kelly collected the cape without trouble and turned to hang it in the closet set aside for the coats of guests.

As she turned back, Kelly drew in a sharp breath, for she found the man leaning in, peering at her from all too close a distance. Brilliant blue eyes narrowed as he regarded her.

"Sir?" Taking a slight step back, but unable to retreat further due to the closet, she offered him another bright, customer-service smile.

"How interesting." Then he leaned back and looked about himself, curiosity radiating with each movement. Upwards, then around. A small snort escaped his nose as he spotted the runic designs – designs that most mundanes thought were affectations – on the pillars and around the ceiling. His lips moved a little, as he read them, as he walked in.

Kelly, freed from the wall, skirted around him and tried to guide him to a nearby table. The old man ignored her, moving ever inwards till he was near the kitchen, and took a seat a short distance from Tobias. He offered the dwarf a familiar, courteous nod as he sat. Eleanor, who was not far away, who had been unnaturally still and as silent as the dead throughout all this, he ignored.

Pointedly.

Seated, arranged at the table, hands steepled, he turned to the kitchen, speaking into it. "Yes, yes. I know your rules. Lily has informed me. Your *guests* are safe."

The sudden chime of a bell indicating service was ready startled Kelly. She jumped a little, even as she finished leading the pair of still-shaken mundanes to their seats near the door. In the way of all humans, though, the threat and worry was already fading, pushed aside and compartmentalized into the farthest reaches of their mind. After all, nothing *actually* happened.

Right?

Depositing the pair, Kelly hurried to the pass-through, where plates of bread and small dishes of salt, butter, olive oil and dark vinegar were spread out. She blinked, staring at the plates, a first in her months working for Mo Meng.

"Boss?"

"Gratis for all who are coming today. We'll be a little slow on service," Mo Meng said, answering her unspoken question. Then a beat, a small, grim smile. "We'll start doing this regularly from now on." He tilted his head upwards, considering. "I'll have to find a proper baker."

"Uhh... sure." She could not help but wonder what a proper baker would be like for the man, while mentally making adjustments to the utensils everyone would need. What she'd have to find. "Okay."

A breath, as she tried to force her mind to stop spinning. Plans, fractured plans going off in a dozen directions, questions left unanswered. Her heart was still beating a rapid tattoo, the almost-altercation from before flooding her body with adrenaline and leaving a bitter, iron taste in her mouth.

"Kelly?" A voice, soft, gentle and yet insistent. It drew her gaze upwards, dilated pupils focused on his. Something in those eyes, an intensity of focus that demanded her entire attention, that focused entirely on her, drew her back, slowed her breathing as she mimicked his own slow and steady rhythm. Gave her a rock to stand upon.

To focus.

She blinked, looked away. Whispered, "Thank you."

"No need."

Gaze fixed on the gleaming pass-through, Kelly focused on the dishes of bread and salt and sides, focused on that moment and rallied, stacking them with consummate skill. Within moments, she was placing bowls of bread and plates of salt and butter on each table. Again and again, she murmured a request for patience, as the kitchen was delayed.

The customers, the regulars, all smiled, nodded. Used to it.

Long fingers tipped with red-lacquered fingernail polish picked up a slice, dipped the buttered bread in salt. Then, Eleanor's gaze never leaving the old man's, she took a small and careful bite, canines and pearlescent teeth flashing.

The crunch of toasted bread, grilled under flame with a hint of char and butter soaked into its soft, white and fluffy center echoed through the restaurant. Little grains of black Hawaiian volcano salt added an additional sharpness to the dish, a pronounced metallic, earthy umami counterpoint to the toast.

The involuntary moan that erupted from Eleanor's mouth was low and sensual. It brought to mind long nights and tossed bedsheets, a flash of crimson splayed across white pillowcases. In the corner, O blinked, blushed. Their newest customers traded long looks, shared smiles dancing on their lips as Kelly arrived with their bread.

Mika took the bread, copying Eleanor's motions as he took a bite. His own expression of pleasure was more silent, his eyes rolling back as the salt flakes crumbled on his tongue and butter filled his mouth.

"Oh come on..." O hissed at their antics. Still, she looked at the dish, the old man, the way the rest of the restaurant was copying those motions. She followed suit, her mouth salivating at the smell. A moment later, she emitted a rather unladylike moan out loud. A hand came up to cover her mouth, though her jaw never stopped moving.

"Salt and bread. How old-fashioned..." Swift motion now, as the old man dipped bread in salt. He admired the dark gold, the black salt flakes contrasting with the bread. The border of crust, the glistening oils. He held the toast, looked around as the other regulars stared at him.

He smiled.

The smell of freshly toasted bread, sugar and wheat and milk, so simple but so profound, had him salivating.

And now...

He took a bite, at last.

Flavor exploded in Merl's mouth, carbon and sulfur and metal and earth and salt and butter and cooked and risen wheat, soft and tender on the inside but with a satisfying crunch as he bit through the toasted outside. A simple ritual, complete.

And the taste...

The taste.

A mouthful, chewing fast. Then another, and another. Dipped in the salt, buttered again with the softened curls, olive oil and vinegar tried next. A different flavor profile, a different taste. No ritual, just food, just bread and butter and common ingredients.

Eaten quickly and then...

Gone.

Done.

Plates empty, all too soon.

The old man frowned, staring at the crumbs left behind. After a moment, he snorted.

"Well played, oh nameless one. By the gift of bread and salt, you have bound me. Better than a kiss, at least."

Wandering by the serving window to deposit additional plates, for the restaurant was filling now, Mo Meng replied, humor lacing every word.

"You've always been a drama queen, Merl." A moment, then he called over his shoulder as he returned to his grill, "Welcome back."

Maui Ribs with Pineapple Marinade

B read enough for the guests, at least for now. He would keep a few warmed and heated, but he was needed back at the grill. He raised the temperature on the hotter side again, moved some of the meat away and set the pieces of chicken aside on a cooking tray to rest. Once he had cleared enough space and moved the now crispy-skinned pieces of chicken to the other side to continue cooking while other, cooked pieces were added to the hotter side after being marinated, he set the tongs aside and hurried the cooked chicken legs over to the warming rack. Those needed to cool and rest, to let the juices be reabsorbed so that when the meat was cut, it would be juicy and tasty.

All done, and still feeling just a tad hurried, Mo Meng was finally ready. Ready for the second main that had to be grilled. Marinated beef ribs, drawn from the fridge and allowed to warm a little to room temperature, sat in large steel containers, submerged in the marinade made earlier in the day.

Beef ribs had a problem. Their tendons, their gristle, were tough. Cooked directly, without further preparation, the tendons and gristle connecting the meat to the bones were unappetizing, unwilling to be parted. It forced a lot of effort from the consumers, making for a less than pleasant meal.

Humanity had come up with numerous methods for dealing with such problems. The most common method was to braise or boil the meat, slow-cooking the ribs to give the tendons time to break down and soften. Smoking the same cuts worked as well, the application of heat over a long period being the important aspect. For that reason, slow cookers had become popular, for the ease that it gave cooking and, importantly, the ability to make 'poor' cuts of meat edible.

There were, however, other methods of breaking down hard tendons and gristle. In this case, the use of an acid – the pineapple juice – that the ribs had been soaking in since the morning would speed up the softening process. This had the added advantage, unlike braising, of keeping the ribs extra moist.

It only worked, of course, on such a short-term basis when the ribs had been sliced thin, no larger than a centimeter and a half at most. If it had been cut into beefier chunks, it would have required significantly more time to get the appropriate level of tenderness.

So, here they were.

Tongs dipped into the steel container, grabbing the long slices of marinated ribs. He pulled the sections of ribs out one by one, marinade dripping, white fat and white ribs glistening down the line as he spread the meat on the grill. He placed it cross-wise to the grill lines, so that it would not fall between them, the constant hiss and spit as the marinade dripped into the flames and coals echoing through the kitchen.

Mo Meng worked fast, lining up ribs all down one side and then the other of the grill before returning to the start, flipping over the first piece of tenderized, marinated meat. Cut so thin, the meat did not require much time at all on the hot grill to cook.

Already he could see the grill marks, the browning of the meat at the edges that spoke of the Maillard reaction. He saw the slight reflective sheen of the glistening fat, the way the meat threatened to curl over further as the tendons tightened as they cooked.

Now he worked with two hands. One flipping the beef over, the second marinating the cooked side. Like with the honey soy chicken, he had to apply the marinade again now, the tender barbecue sauce, when it was already cooked, rather than while it was cooking.

Under the heat, the sugars – from the brown sugar, from the molasses – melted, caramelized, and sweetened the meat. The fish sauce deepened the taste, the soy sauce adding a boost of umami and saltiness.

One side done, the meat finished, he went back to the start. He turned the long strips of beef ribs over again, easier now as the meat no longer flopped. Marinade was added once more, a quick brush-down with one hand as the other flipped more ribs. Hands flew across the grill now, as conversations and concerns outside the kitchen faded.

Mo Meng could not spare any attention for the troubles of the restaurant, the clash of energies outside, the cut-glass tension of his customers. It was why he loved cooking, this requirement of his complete attention. When even a moment's distraction could mean failure.

If he mistimed this, the meat would shift from glazed and sweet to burnt and crispy.

And what a tragedy that would be.

Grove Tender

Outside, tensions had risen once more. A new regular had arrived, nodding genially to Kelly as he entered, focused on his table at the back. For a man so large that he had to duck when he stepped through the doors, he was slow in assessing the situation. Slow in spotting the newcomer. When he spotted him, he was slow in making a decision, slow to act. But he did so anyway, changing course.

"You." Jotun's voice rumbled as he loomed over the old man's – Merl's – table. He stared down at the other, brows drawn down and creasing the blond giant's face. "I thought you slept."

"I did, but an annoying woman came and woke me," Merl said, unperturbed by the other's presence.

"Just because we traded spells long ago, and we might be distantly – very distantly – related, she came flouncing in, with no care for manners or courtesy, and pestered me to rise."

"Would you have preferred to sleep, old one?" Tobias said curiously as he turned in his seat. Hands, big, almost comically oversized hands, scarred and weathered, were clasped around his stomach. "I'd heard your rest was involuntary."

"For the first few hundred years, I might have raged. After that, it was quite peaceful. The whispers stopped, back then." Now Merl touched his temple with two fingers, as though he heard that voice even now. He smiled a little as he looked upwards, eyes resting on the embedded runes. "There's not many places I can go, where it's quiet."

The dwarf tapped his foot on the ground, sinking the tips of steel-toed boots into the concrete floor and sending a ringing noise through the restaurant. Once, twice and a third time, he repeated the action. In a corner, another pair of guests, bearded and stocky, echoed his actions. Other guests looked askance or bemused, a raven-haired woman pausing in the midst of setting up her camera and cords and cursing under her breath at missing the event.

"May the walls hold," Tobias murmured, a quiet echo following his words to end the ritual.

Kelly, coming up by the influencer, smiled down at her as she set a glass of water on the table. "No filming."

"But..."

"No filming. Or we'll ask you to leave."

Pouting a bit, the woman began to pack her items away. However, when Kelly turned her back, she pulled out her phone, holding it as though she was going to play on it. It flicked on, and then, after a moment, went blank, causing her to frown.

A short distance away, O smirked as she slipped a small pen-like object back into her breast pocket.

Kelly, having dealt with the influencer for the moment, came over to stand beside Tobias, arms crossed.

"You know you shouldn't do that!"

"That one alluded to things that should not be spoken of," Tobias said solemnly. "Ritual must be observed."

Eyeing the cracked concrete, the waitress sighed. "Did it have to include breaking our floor?"

"Mo Meng should reinforce it, if he intends to host deep dwellers."

Merl raised a hand, cutting Kelly off before she could continue their argument. "Leave the child of earth alone. His kind are old and unwilling to change."

"His kind?" O muttered. "He doesn't mean boomers, does he?"

Mika snorted, then hid his moment of amusement behind a glass of water.

"Not as old as you," the dwarf grumbled.

Kelly shook her head, then eyed the various mortal guests who were looking a little surprised and curious at the interactions. She hurried over, plastering a friendly smile on her face that morphed into her usual cheerfulness moments later as she discussed drinks and meals with the guests, distracting them. When asked what the problem was by a pair of wide-eyed Americans, she shrugged and faux-whispered, 'Foreigners'. That shut them up. It even had the advantage of being entirely truthful, for neither Tobias or Merl was from Canada originally.

In the center of the room, O and Mika were regarding the giant who continued to loom over Merl, waiting to be spoken to again. He was a silent and ominous presence, for Mika was hiding the flickering lights on his beeper which were, slowly, receding in intensity.

Leaning over, O whispered to her companion. "Is that...?"

"Yeah."

"Shit."

"Yeah."

"Why not return to sleeping, then?" Jotun rumbled when Merl looked back at him.

"She might have hinted that there were changes – vast changes – that I had to see." A lip quirked into a wry smile. "Over and above the introduction of chimneys."

"And has it been worthwhile? This search?"

"Yes." A hand ran through white hair, pulling at the mohawk; then he grinned. "Do you know what a silver fox is?"

"Oh no," Eleanor breathed out, in a tone of horror. She placed a hand over her face, unwilling to look at the old man any further. Some men just never learned.

"I do not," Jotun rumbled. "Is that what you intend then, grove tender?"

"Among other things." His voice dropped as he continued. "Funny you should use that old title. There's not many groves left, not on the Emerald Isles. Might have to see about changing that."

This caused the pair of DESE agents to twitch, visibly. Kelly, wandering by with plates of bread for a newcomer, stopped for a brief moment, looking at the pair and then the regulars, from the wide-eyed Eleanor to the frowning Jotun.

"Jotun, you should consider sitting down. And ordering," she added. "Mo Meng mentioned there's only a limited number of servings of ribs today. Same with the dessert, so if you want your usual multiple orders, I'll need it soon." Then she turned to Merl. "More bread?"

"Yes, wench."

Eyes narrowed, then a single finger rose in front of his face. "No."

"What do you mean?"

"We don't do 'wench' or 'babe' or 'honey' or anything else like that. I gave you my name when you came in." She tapped her shirt where she'd pinned a nametag. "It's here too if you can't remember. That works. Or Miss."

"But that is your station," said Merl.

"Again. No. We aren't America to blather on about our various freedoms, but we don't do stations or classes or other things like that." A little chuckle. "Even if we do have a king, we don't really offer him much fealty or loyalty in this country. Certainly not any obeisance."

"I would not either. He's not the True King," Merl said.

"Ah, yes. Charlemagne. We still wait for him," Eleanor said with a smile. She could not help but interject, just to see the man's reaction.

Merl twitched, tilted his head to the side, then ignored her, refusing to rise to the bait.

"Miss Kelly. Thank you. I shall sit. And yes, multiple orders. Two each of whatever he has," Jotun said, turning to his table. He had taken a step away before he spun around, eyebrows snapping down as he spoke, his voice a low rumble. "Watch more, act slow. This world has not been kind to us. It is more complicated by far than the one you remember."

All he received in answer was a smile from the old man.

With Jotun seated, Kelly moved on to the next source of trouble, depositing plates of bread and salt, taking orders and heading back to the pass-through. Ears attuned to the ebb and flow of the conversations around her, she worked the floor to ensure everyone had their orders. She looked up as the door swung open and more customers arrived.

Another two parties, together. And only enough tables for one group. With a shake of her head, she shifted direction a little to the closet and board to begin a waiting list.

Maybe she really had done too good a job promoting the restaurant.

The First Plate

M o Meng was done. The ribs were finished, the heat on the grill lowered. He had another big metal serving platter for later, but for now, he had enough to begin plating the first orders. The chicken was still resting, needing a little more time before he was ready to plate it. The beef ribs, on the other hand, could just go; they were thin enough that the amount of juice lost would be minimal.

To start, he would have to deal with the corn. He rotated the corn, shucking the ones that need shucking and turning the others so that they could continue to cook on the grill. The ones that were finished, he placed on a new serving tray, shifting the older one with the corn that had cooled a little away.

Those, he took with him to the cutting board and got to work with a cleaver. Ends were taken off, the corn sliced into inch-and-a-half portions so that they were easy to pick up or strip with a knife and fork. He could have left them whole, but then Kelly would have to run about getting more napkins for everyone, and that was unfair to her. So instead he sliced them into smaller portions before they were placed on their plates.

Mashed potatoes went on next, in one corner of each of the dozen plates he'd laid out. Then the coleslaw next to the potatoes. He took his time with the coleslaw, ensuring that the scoops came up with the slaw, but not too much of the liquid. Down the center, the pieces of chopped corn, separating the coleslaw and mashed potatoes.

Finally, the mains.

Five pieces of the Maui ribs, three or four ribs apiece. Each slice was nearly a foot long, but sliced thin, and glistening from the fats and caramelized sugar as it cooked over the grill. The smell filled his nostrils, of mashed potatoes and cream and barbecue sauce and grilled meat, tempting him to taste again.

But he'd done enough of that, as he cooked. This was for his customers.

Plate after plate was completed before it was placed on the pass-through, the bell tapped to summon his trusty waitress. A waitress who was looking increasingly harried as she added another name to the waiting list, offered a smile and an apology to the man standing there before she hurried over to a patron who was asking for more water.

A quick look back at the grill. He twitched his finger, pulling energy and sending it over the grill, holding back the heat for a moment. That done, Mo Meng picked up the last few plates, trekking out of the swinging doors that separated his domain from the restaurant itself.

It reminded him of older times. Better times, perhaps. Before she had arrived, when he might have a half-dozen customers the whole day, and he could serve them singly. Now he carried the plates to his customers, to help his employee.

Service in order of arrival, of course.

Over by their table, the first customers of the day were in hushed conversation, heads bent as they whispered to one another.

O was speaking hurriedly. "What do we do? He can't be intending to regrow the forests over existing cities, right? That's, like, eco-terrorism."

"We do nothing. That's what the Mage Council is for. We'll let them know and let them handle it," Mika answered. "Remember, we're here to watch and learn too."

"But..."

"No buts!"

"Definitely not in my restaurant," Mo Meng said with a smile as he placed the dishes in front of them. "Two orders of the Maui ribs. That's correct, right?"

There was a slight hesitation as O looked at the meal, then at Mika who was already nodding agreeably. He pulled his plate toward him as he continued. "Thank you, chef."

"Chef." Mo Meng mouthed the word, then nodded. "A good enough title, for now. Better than others I've had, at least."

"Well, we might..." O cut off with a hiss after being kicked under the table.

Not that Mo Meng paid any attention to their horseplay. Just before he left, he gestured at Merl who was working his way through a second basket of bread. "If you pay attention this night, you might find your answer already present."

Then, having said his piece, he walked off to help Kelly further. She was busy rushing plates back and forth, even while glancing worriedly into the empty kitchen. Afte all, most diners in groups had ordered a variety of dishes.

"What's he mean?" O hissed.

Mika waved a hand to hush his partner. She eventually turned to look at Merl too, though her hands – like his – moved to cut and split the ribs as she peered about. No need to make their observation too obvious.

Not that the man was doing anything interesting at the moment. Who looked at a clear glass of water that closely, holding it barely an inch from his eyes as he turned it around and around? Surely filtered water was not that fascinating.

Distracted, she popped the piece of meat she'd cut free into her mouth with little thought. As she turned away, to look at the other diners, she froze halfway through the motion. Finally the smell, the taste of her meal had registered.

Sweet. The Maui rib marinade was laced with brown sugar and molasses which was then caramelized, so it was sweet. That was the first, obvious layer. Right underneath that, paired with the sweetness, was the acidity of the pineapple and the tartness of the fruit. Caramel and cinnamon and the taste of smoke and charcoal, all embedded in the beefiness of the meat, filled her mouth, her nose as she chewed.

The ribs were chewy, but the good kind, the kind where the meat fell off the bones but still required you to work a little, crushing and tearing to release more juices. Just enough tension that you had to work for it a little, to savor the taste and feel in your mouth.

She chewed, the taste of the ribs filling her mouth, catching her attention fully. Stopped the parts of her that kept questioning the presence of the regulars, made the fear and nervousness that she'd been trying to conceal with action freeze. Made her pay attention to what she was eating. And then, suddenly, the bite was gone, sliding down her throat with casual ease.

Leaving her bereft, but a plate full of sides before her. Like the mashed potatoes.

Creamy goodness, the potatoes smooth and velvety in her mouth, the butter and cream pairing with the lingering taste of the ribs and effortlessly soaking it in. She chewed and swallowed by reflex, dipping a fork into the coleslaw.

Light and refreshing, slightly tangy. The smell of cream and milk and fresh vegetables, all mixed together. Not too heavy to overshadow the rest of the dish, but cold and refreshing to cleanse the mouth. A dish to be paired with everything else, even as one cut across the corn and sawed down the edges, to part the corn from the cob. The taste of charcoal and butter with fresh corn, sweet and crunchy. So sweet, and just a bit starchier than she had expected.

Eyes wide, she took another bite, registered that she was right the first time. This was no mass market corn, but something that had been grown by hand, an heirloom piece that a farmer sold at a farmer's market or kept for himself. Never enough to feed everyone, but that wasn't the point.

The point was the taste, the care that had been taken, the way it all worked together.

Knife and fork dipped, mixing beef and coleslaw and corn together for another bite, testing the differences. Three sides, one main. Not infinite variations, but enough that she knew she could never try them all before the meal was done.

But she'd try.

Another mouthful of bliss.

And another.

As a bubble of silence descended over the eaters, while those still waiting looked on enviously.

The Right Kind of Magic

Kelly smiled, watching magic happen once again. That was the thing about the Nameless Restaurant. The ceilings might be filled with runes, magic might run in the very bones of the building, but the real magic ...that happened in the kitchen, with nothing more than fire and blade and attention to detail.

She busied herself around the tables, helping to deliver the last of the Maui ribs. She filled glasses, hurrying to the door and taking names as the crowd that stood outside grew. Now that food was arriving, she knew the customers would rotate faster, the mundanes moving on after finishing their meals while the regulars lingered, ordering additional dishes, conversing among themselves or over one another, and finally partaking of the dessert. Some of the mundanes, though, they'd eat and leave, missing out on the finale.

A pity, but it was not her job to dictate their dining habits.

Just to serve.

"More water, sir?" Kelly said, holding up the pitcher toward the old man.

"Yes...w-... woman?" Merl said, hesitating.

"Better. 'Miss' works. Or 'Kelly' would be even better. I like my friends calling me that," Kelly said brightly.

"And we are friends?" Merl looked amused, as he used a forkful of mashed potatoes to scoop up escaped beef juices from his plate. "Few would dare such thoughts so quickly."

"Really? I'm surprised. You have a nice smile, after all," Kelly said as she finished refilling his glass. "Anything else I can do for you?"

"There is more to come, yes?"

"The rest of your order. Chicken and dessert."

"Then I am well."

"Just holler if you need me, then." So saying, Kelly moved away, leaving Merl to finish mopping the rest of his plate. She passed by Jotun's table, picking up one of the empty plates as she passed by before refilling his glass.

Always moving, nodding amiably to Eleanor who was taking her time with her meal. She always ate slowly and gracefully, savoring each bite as though she had all the time in the world. She noted that the lady had extra meat and no coleslaw on her plate as requested, while Tobias was still working on his meal. Each plate, each rib carefully sliced apart and proportioned, each mouthful of mashed potatoes carefully shaped and compacted before it made its way into his mouth.

Mortal customers ate as well, some of those waiting at the doorway looking on impatiently. The pair that had arrived early were sharing a single plate of ribs, having a long conversation about a recent office scandal. The influencer with their phone out was eating with one hand, tapping and fiddling with it in a desperate attempt to get the expensive piece of equipment to work. An older gentleman, having finished his meal, was waving for the bill, head bent over a weathered book. She rung him up, leaving him the credit card machine before she went for the door.

The crowd outside grew in volume as she came over, holding her clipboard. She took more names, frowning a little at the line that was standing beside the dumpster, that lingered smoking across the lone streetlight.

"How much longer?" a pair of young femmes asked. Not unkindly, but impatiently. They licked their lips, as a gust of air brought delectable smells out of the building.

Kelly paused, running through her guest list and their orders. Then she tacked on a generous addition of time. "Another forty to fifty minutes, I think."

"That long?" the pixie-cut, petite leader said, exasperated.

"We're not really a fast-dining restaurant," Kelly replied, offering the other a sympathetic smile. "Our customers like to enjoy their meals."

"I can see that," the brunette of the pair said, long hooked nose set in a delicate heart-shaped face. "And some of them really like their food."

"Some of our regulars do enjoy eating, yes." Kelly smiled, stepping back to begin disengagement.

"Who does your interior design?" the brunette asked, curiously. "The sound muffling is amazing. Even with the door open, I can barely hear anything."

"I... do not know." Kelly replied, tilting her head back. While it was not as though she could pick out individual conversations from here at the door, it did not seem remarkable to her. Then, curiously, she looked upward. New runes, scribbled along the walls, had appeared. They were always appearing, changing, shifting.

Had her boss done something different? Made preparations for their new clientele?

"Well, compliments to him. Though this Nordic rune thing, it's a little dated."

"It's not..." Kelly began to correct her, then shook her head. "I'll let you know when we have a table." She offered them another smile and wave, retrieved her clipboard from the latest in the line, and made her way away, dropping the waiting list in its spot beside the stairs as she left.

A quick trip to the table, glancing at the card machine and the receipt as she confirmed the dining experience had been pleasant. No answer, just an absent nod, as the man stood up. She didn't mind. He might not be a *regular* regular, but the bookworm was becoming a consistent customer, always with a book. Ate fast, tipped well, never spoke to anyone as he read.

Tucking the debit card machine in her apron, she pulled out a rag and cleaned the table. Curiosity niggled at her, and she considered her options. Knowledgeable as the regulars might be, none were mages. Some dabbled, of course, but it was not a specialty. Merl was an unknown, though she had suspicions about him.

On the other hand, there were two newcomers, newcomers who were paid to know.

Table cleaned, she called for the next in line, ushered them over. Provided them the menu, took their orders and got them their drinks. Waited on a few more tables, dropped off new plates, with Mo Meng finally back in the kitchen. She hurried about, dealing with her customers till she found a moment to stop next to the pair.

O's meal was done and she was looking longingly at her partner's plates. Mika was taking his time to enjoy his meal, seemingly oblivious to the hungry eyes beside him. When Kelly arrived, jug of water in hand, he offered her a smile as she refilled their glasses. Then frowned, when she stayed.

"I have a question," Kelly said. "If you don't mind me asking."

"Depends on the question," O said.

"It's a simple one that I think you might have an answer for." She nodded over to the entrance where a pair waited, and caught sight of another couple at a table waving for her. Kelly offered the couple a nod; the man clutched the girl's hand possessively, his attention returning to his partner the moment she acknowledged them.

Best to get them a check soon. It seemed they had plans.

"Well?" O said, impatiently.

"Are magical – supernatural – conversations being muffled?" Kelly said, bluntly.

"Of course not," O said, scornfully. At the same time, Mika was shaking his head and frowning.

Focusing on the man, Kelly waited for more details.

"It's very complicated magic to filter for keywords. Almost impossible, really, because it's so easy to change things around. Worse, because you then have to decide how much of a conversation to dull or mute." Mika glanced towards the kitchen where Mo Meng worked before he added, "I'm sure he could do it, but... it's not worth it."

O snorted. "What I said."

"So he's probably just masking all conversations from those who aren't magically active," Mika said. "Using wards of intent and focus, to direct the conversation."

O blinked, surprised at Mika's acknowledgment of magic and change. Kelly, catching sight of a second glance the impatient couple shot her way, nodded thanks.

Curiosity was assuaged, for now.

As for the details, that was for others who had the gift.

She was just a server.

A Simple Meal

T he heart of a meal was not the ingredients. It was not even the technique or the recipe. It was in the satisfaction of the consumer. Not the crass, modern version of the word, but the old definition: the individual who consumes, the one who eats. They who take in and enjoy the meal, in its entirety or in portions; but who leave happy.

The chicken legs fully rested, Mo Meng took a moment to check the internal temperature of one with a simple meat thermometer before he threw them back onto the barbecue. He had a brush at the ready and the earlier soy marinade on-hand, so that he could brush the chicken legs down one last time. This time, the chicken and glaze would be left for only a few minutes, long enough to warm up and for the sugars to caramelize a little further, and then the dish would finally be ready.

He did that for a dozen orders as he listened to the slight sizzle of juices forced out, of his marinade striking the coals, of the whirl of the fan above. A breath in and the smell of cooking meat, caramelizing sugars and the slight tang of soy sauce filled the air, so thick he could swear he could see it.

Then he was done and plating. Pulling chicken off onto the side, checking a particularly large drumstick with the meat thermometer. Better to be sure, better to be certain. True, he could trust his instincts, his years of experience with this kitchen and with cooking. But why bother, when one had a simple new tool to do the same?

Easier than casting a spell, more certain than the touch test or experience. There were simple tools and conveniences in the modern age that even the most powerful magician had never experienced in their most private of sanctums.

Warm water? Of course. Easy enough to cast a spell and warm a bowl or bath.

Weather resistant clothing? An easy enchantment on the weave to improve cloaks and shirts.

Illumination, late into the night? Fairy lights or spirit gems or balls of infused Mana.

All these things they had, but others? No. After all, powerful magicians they might be, but the power of imagination, of a network of minds working towards luxury for all, could not be beat. Obviously, the Internet and computers were the most obvious results, but it was the smaller, simpler things that Mo Meng treasured.

Humidifiers to add moisture to the air.

Air purifiers, to clear it of lingering smells.

Deodorant provided to the masses, so that walking medieval city streets might not be a chore.

Regular dental care.

Mass-manufactured clothing. So much that it had become a problem; clothing – clothing made of cotton and wool, work that once would have taken weeks and months to produce – was now cast aside in container-loads.

Even the idea of container ships, storage in large ocean-going vessels, bringing trade goods on a daily, even hourly basis, was amazing. Not just spices or tea or other bulk and expensive commodities, but perishables like bananas and pears and corn and children's toys.

The modern world was a marvel, one that Mo Meng tried to ensure he took in with proper awe and respect. It was all too easy, even for him, to get used to such wonders. To take for granted hot, running water and access to spices the world over. Too easy, at times, to retreat in fear at all this change, all these marvels that staggered the imagination.

Or to dismiss them, as silly tricks and mere baubles.

Sometimes it took time and a proper mindset to understand the world as it was.

The good, the bad, the foolish and the routine.

In the meantime, he had dinner to cook, plates to finish and a barbecue to tend.

Hands moved across the grill, shifting legs to waiting plates, setting them aside in rows before he switched, cleaning off the grill before he added the next round of beef ribs. He would have to work fast, to ensure the beef was not burned before he returned.

Plating for this dish was not elaborate. Sides were the same as before, all ready to be spooned onto the waiting dishes. There had been little reason to add additional workload. Perhaps another time, he might consider another, lighter and less creamy salad. Something simple, with raisins for additional sweetness and walnuts for crunch; but he was alone back here and even experience could not alter the constraints of time and space.

Not without more magic than he was willing to employ.

He never stopped moving, eyes flicking over the receipts, checking quantities and amendments. Adding dishes to the pass-through and shifting some around, so that plates could be served at the same time for waiting diners.

It was not perfect. Some of the ribs had cooled a little, even under the warming lights. The chicken had not enough time to rest, after being warmed again, some of the ribs too long. It was not perfect, not anymore. It grated on his nerves, just a little; this alteration in his routine.

He could, would do something about it. For now, it was good enough.

At least till the teething problems of their sudden popularity were dealt with.

Kelly swept up the newly delivered plates with practiced ease, carrying the dishes over to a couple. As she crossed the floor, she could sense the sudden spike of interest, the way diners focused upon her. By this point, she was used to it, though it was a little more intense than before.

She placed the plates before the couple, two sets of barbecued chicken legs with accompanying sides, and smiled as the customers caught a whiff of their meal. A slight dilation of pupils, the pair leaning forwards and grasping utensils. They barely acknowledged her question about additional condiments, so focused were they. She had to move on, though, now that the dishes were arriving.

More plates of chicken arrived at the regular tables, one each to the diners to start with. She knew better than to drop off an entire order, even if it was multiples of the same thing. Too much of the dish would cool before the diners could get to it. Merl received his second plate of the night, a fact that had him frowning a little, but she ignored it.

Some customers, you just had to be rude to.

Kelly was doing math in her head – table turnover math. The restaurant regulars would take their time, lingering. Unlike Mo Meng, she had to deal with the waiting crowd, so better to turn over the tables faster. That meant getting plates to the mortals who were further away and would finish fast. It was only a matter of minutes, but sometimes minutes mattered.

Especially as dessert orders started coming in.

More than that, letting them start first would make them happy. She'd get a better tip, and knowing the regulars, it'd be in cash. Four-leaf clovers were great for saving one from a falling flowerpot, not so much for paying the rent.

Head down, feet moving swiftly, she kept picking up plates and depositing them as she went along, removing tickets as she cleared them and adding a few more. Once the ready plates were cleared, she had checks to finish, tables to clean and new customers to greet. Some mundane, a few magical, and others harder to classify. Particularly interesting were the reactions of the supernatural, newcomers and regulars alike, who made it through the wards for their seats.

Who they reacted to was of interest to Kelly, though more as an academic matter. Some noted Eleanor or Jotun, and then moved on. The regulars barely even acknowledged those two. The DESE agents, sitting quietly and having dinner, made a few reconsider their meal. Yet it was Merl, that old man, who caused the greatest disruption. That old man separating his chicken leg with gusto into bite-sized pieces, his presence was a disruption. Those who saw him – truly saw him – blanched, retreated and left, before she could get a word in.

That helped a little with the line. The mundanes either barely noticed or noticed and moved on. That was the human condition, the social contract – to ignore events and people that were not their business. Little graces, for children weeping over fallen ice cream or an ill-timed slip. Little grotesqueries, when tragedies played out in front of others; a weeping woman, a struggling man. A quiet, civil, city contract that in another situation might have been disastrous, but right now, just made things easier for her.

Then again, that was the point of the contract.

In the meantime, Merl was eating, separating off long strips of meat with his utensils. Occasionally, he'd stop and turn over the knife in his hand, shaking his head a little with contained amusement. Steel worth a king's fortune, unstained and spotless, provided to every commoner and peasant for their use.

What a marvel.

What a foolish waste.

Then, wonder and distraction would cease as the smell of fresh grilled meat, of honey and a more concentrated, slightly sour scent would reach him. Not the sides, which he had tasted before and still enjoyed; though perhaps it was a touch heavier on the cream than he preferred. It certainly missed a bite that he was used to from fresh milk.

Then again, for all the vibrancy in the meals, all the variety of new spices and fruits and vegetables available, he had also found a consistency to things, a lack of randomness that he missed in so many meals. This modern world worshipped so often at the altar of consistency that apples were available by the truckload, but all of them of the same kind.

All of them similar.

No matter if he traveled in his own lands, lands that he had to leave because aching familiarity was gone, replaced by the ringing emptiness of a lost limb. No matter if he went to a new country, to the one over the sea or the ocean.

It was still missing.

The trees, the great forests of the old world that stretched for miles and swallowed individuals without a whisper? The groves that he and his master had studied in, where knowledge had been carved into bark and memory woven into cords hung from branches? Where were the plinths and hedges, the places of worship he had known?

Gone.

Replaced by shopping malls and open pastures, by bleating sheep not in the tens or hundreds but in thousands. Scrubland that was fenced off for farmers who complained about immigrants, as though these Saxons and Normans were not themselves invaders of his fair isle.

A world of wonder and wisdom, giving way to rolling fields of boredom and regularity. He had to leave, before a heart once frozen was torn apart again. Better to see new countries, new kingdoms, to chase after an elusive jinn for answers. Better to leave, before he broke faith with his king.

Only to find himself here.

Meeting a man he'd only ever known in dreams, trapped as he was. Though the dreams of an Archmage were not the dreams of your regular person. To taste food cooked by another, not with illusion or enchantment or conjured from leaves and flowers and promises, but by hand and sweat.

To find that even now, a mortal hand could make food as divine as the fae's trickery.

Given time, given practice, given care.

Honey-glazed meat, cooked on an open flame with a touch of smoke still on it. A reminder of meals he had eaten so long ago. Meals shared with the greatest of men, those who had placed the needs of others above their own. Meals with those who had accepted him, for all his numerous flaws – inborn and chosen alike.

A meal filled with memory, but not charred and burnt, nor overcooked and dry on one side. A meal filled with new tastes, texture and depth that his own memories lacked.

Sweetness paired with a slight spice and an intensity of flavor that he was not used to. A sweet heat, unlike the peppers they had once used, or the sharp green taste of dill. The honey brought out the tenderness of the chicken, the thighs a little fatty and the drumsticks a moist mouthful, the skin crackling under his teeth at each bite.

Then, mashed potatoes. Except he had never realized that without the slight sourness of pineapple and heaviness of beef, the sweetness here was more delicate. The mash brought out the more pronounced flavors of the honey in the chicken, added to the creaminess of the meal he was swallowing and cooled the heat of the dish.

Another bite of chicken, as his mouth flooded with saliva and his eyes widened, his concerns about those behind and around fading for a moment. Combine the new bite with coleslaw, chilled as it was, creamy and crunchy at the same time, fresh vegetables and a cooling presence that cleared his tastebuds and drew another bite.

A simple meal, elevated by herbs and care and spiced with memories of the past. Good memories, the best kind.

Even if memories were all he had.

A Slice of Cake

K elly deposited plates of dessert at another table, checking in with the trio of tikbalang. They looked the same as any mortal, thanks to the glamours they used, the charms hanging off their wrists. Maybe a little longer in the face, a little more muscular than average. They had a youngster with them, a teenager. Cute kid who, outside of stopping to eat, was constantly on his phone. A quick check made sure they were fine before she moved on, heading for Merl's table as she spotted the empty plate. As she neared, she noted the morose look on the older man's face.

She'd turned over a few tables by now, individuals who had eaten quickly and finished before the others, or others who were skipping dessert. The majority were supernaturals who were looking for a meal and finding the environment a little more restrictive than normal—whether it was because of the DESE or the old man.

Good tips, so far, except for the pair of businessmen. Why was it, that the richest were the meanest when it came to tips? Oh, there were the occasional exceptions, but they were uncommon. If she saw a suit, if she wasn't working a nightclub, well, she'd expect the worst possible tips —apart from the Sunday afternoon church crowd. Thankfully, the Nameless Restaurant did not cater to that group.

She wondered how the old man would tip. If he would.

"Was everything to your satisfaction?" Kelly asked as she cleared the table. It was a rote question, but it seemed to break the older man out of his thoughts.

"Well enough," Merl said. "The food was, certainly." He opened his mouth, then shut it with a small shake of his head.

She could ask. She might have with a regular. But he was not one, and no matter what Mo Meng said, she was not sure if she wanted him to be. There was an edge to the older man, beyond his casual old-fashioned misogyny, that put her back up. She occasionally noticed the same thing with some of the other diners, the older ones in particular.

"Dessert?" she said instead.

"Of course. I might as well," Merl said, amused. "She did say that it was all to die for. I might as well try it all."

"I'll bring it right out." She left for the doors, picking up a few more plates on the way and verifying dessert orders as she did so. Dirty dishes were deposited as she stepped into the kitchen, noting the growing pile there. They'd need someone to work the dishes, if things got much busier. She doubted Mo Meng had enough dishes – though perhaps he did. Sometimes it felt like his pantry was larger on the inside than it had any right to be.

Paperwork, notes and receipts started printing out. She cleaned her hands quickly, went to where the desserts had been set to cool. She slid the first tray out, swiftly cutting the cakes into squares. Each square contained a full ring of pineapple with some space in between. As she worked, she caught the scent of the moist cake, melted sugar – so much sugar – and butter, cinnamon in the cake and, of course, the gleaming caramelized frosting over the succulent pineapple slice.

She should have stolen a piece earlier for herself. If they ran out, she would be quite upset.

To her surprise, Merl had a visitor. Not O, who was seated glowering in her chair, but Mika. To a casual viewer he might look perfectly at ease, but from her angle she could see the hand clutching his knee in a white-knuckled grip.

"We're an international governmental organization tasked with the supervision, management and aid of supernaturals. One of the tasks we undertake is the... orientation of individuals to the modern world," Mika was saying. "We also do regular briefing sessions about changing laws, provide details of where one might find glamour enchantments and even aid in job searches."

"A job? I have one. I am the One True King's magical advisor."

"Of course, of course. But he hasn't arisen yet, has he? And in the meantime, modern jobs provide modern payment methods. I'm sure you've noticed the use of them."

"I already have those pieces of paper you use for money." With a flourish, Merl pulled a wad of bills out and waved it at Mika. "See."

"Well, yes." Mika eyed the bills, then gently pointed out, "But those are rupees. And we're in Canada."

"Are they?" He rubbed his fingers together to make the bills shift, and color began to ripple up the dull-colored notes. Material and size changed, as reds and blues took over. "Done."

"That's... you can't!" O cried from her seat. "That's not legal."

"The merchants were happy to take them."

"Because they thought they were real," Mika said, tiredly. "Fae coin is deeply frowned upon. Surely you had the same problem, in your time?"

"This is not fae coin," Merl said, dangerously. "Do not compare me – or my magic – to them. What I give will not disappear or change after the day has dawned." He tapped the edges of the paper against the table. "This is no different, though I must admit, this new... 'plastic' is strange. Difficult at first to replicate."

"We really could do with less of it in the world," Kelly couldn't help but mutter to herself as she neared.

Mika pursed his lips, cast a glance at Kelly and shook his head. She kept her mouth shut at his silent plea, even as he fished in his pockets and pulled out a bill of his own. "I did not mean that. But surely you realise you are not the only individual of power. Those papers are not just, well, paper. Or plastic in our case. Many have different aspects."

"Are you saying my magic is inadequate?" Merl muttered, dangerously.

"Of course not. I would not dare." Quite literally, Kelly assumed. After all, if he gripped his knee any harder, he'd either break his fingers or draw blood. As it was, she was certain he was going to have quite the bruise. "Just that you might not be aware of things to make your magic as effective as it could be."

Wrinkles deepened as Merl frowned at Mika. Before he could reply, Kelly dropped two plates of pineapple upside down cake on the table with a slight thunk. Turning her head, she winked at Mika, knowing he had not ordered a piece. Still, if she'd learned one thing about old monsters in her time here, it was that they were easily bribed.

At least with Mo Meng's dishes.

"Tell me more…" Merl said slowly, eyeing Mika's plate with avaricious cunning.

Kelly snorted but moved on. A small enough price, a piece of cake, if it made an old man listen.

The First Bite

Merl shifted in irritation, splitting his attention again to listen to the droning bureaucrat. This modern world was so strange, to give power to men of papers rather than warriors and teachers, to those who preached rather than those who served and ruled.

Stranger still, they had split up the tasks that he was once responsible for into individual organizations. Wise men no longer spoke on multiple subjects, their every word listened to and considered. Instead, their advice was slipped into reams of dead trees, kept partitioned in buildings that any foolish, stumble-fingered fool with a candle could enter, and in ill-conceived, glaring, unnatural rectangles that displayed lore from around the world. They listened to talking heads blaring over metal speakers, sought advice from those who – often badly – tried to distill difficult concepts into thirty-second, witty comments.

As though everyone had the right to be a bard.

So many speakers, so many advice-makers, all of it mixed in with preachers of every variety. Common sense being passed on as words of great wisdom, and sometimes, it felt like it.

Why would you need to tell people to take a walk through the woods? To eat when hungry? To bend the knee and aid those who had fallen, for they were all part of your clan. To take up arms against those that weren't.

Yet that too was wrong... So perhaps common wisdom was no longer common, nor perhaps wisdom.

For clans intermixed, and strangers abounded.

So advice abounded, like what this man spoke. Advice not just about the important things – like when to plant, what to plant and when to harvest – but also on how to raise children and what punishments to mete out when laws were broken. Advice on the practical, and strange concepts, like this compound interest. On money, whose value was a shared delusion that paper or plastic or dots on a screen were actually worth something, unlike the cow that gave milk or the land one stood upon.

Slips of paper and more virtual tokens of ownership for companies that chased him from country to country; companies that polluted the waterways and tore down trees, but none chose to acknowledge ownership and responsibility. Acts of great malice and malevolence conducted under the guise of shared responsibility. Shared across workers and supervisors and owners, so that they did what they would, only caring when overworked lawmen came for them.

And even then, perhaps not. As the land shrieked and the people cried.

Like absent lords who'd raised rents till their serfs could no longer eat, so that his liege had to take action and cast them down in punishment.

Most of all, he could not understand how they could all be so foolish.

Even the meanest of them had a breadth of knowledge that staggered his imagination. Their experts were skillful and knowledgeable, able to discern details of the world even the greatest magicians of his time had not known. How could they? Such knowledge was collected by thousands, hundreds of thousands of individuals working together, using magic – nay, science – that they had never envisioned.

Years of study, like his own peers had once undertaken, but often on single subjects. And education, provided to even the basest child in these towering and crowded cities of the west.

And still, they were just as foolish – perhaps more so -- as the meanest of those in the southern continents who had no such access. They raped and pillaged the earth and made up laws about corporations, to do the same again.

How foolish, for a society that had enough wealth that such largesse was possible. And so few cared, even as they garnered the knowledge and skills to survive this twisted and altered world. Training offered not by parents or neighbors but by impersonal teachers, so that they could learn and sometimes, specialize in their area of study.

Yet, so few ever found their passion like the man in the kitchen.

Then again, had it not taken him centuries?

Perhaps that was the tragedy, that so few had time. Though even that, these modern mayflies were intent on fighting.

"What was this called again?" Merl asked, looking up for that outspoken woman. If she had red hair, he'd know why. Even that he could not trust in, though, for this world basked in everyday illusions, hiding truth behind glamour over and over again.

"Pineapple upside down cake," Mika said smoothly, pausing his explanation about the programs available from DESE. "The fruit on top is the pineapple. It's a tropical fruit."

"I know that." Admittedly, Merl had only learned that fact a month ago, never having seen the fruit before. Spending a day in that supermarket had been fascinating, though learning to consume the various fruits and vegetables had been a task and a half. "And he cooked it. How interesting."

Taking that as acknowledgment that he could continue, Mika switched back to the topic he had been harping on. A portion of Merl's mind continued to file the details away, continued to test the magic and perfect his own bills as he studied the real bills set alongside it. It seemed the art of forgery and tricks had taken quite a step forward, along with the necessary magical safeguards to detect such actions.

Who knew? There might be central deposits of such slips of paper where spells were cast, detecting fluctuations in magical density.

Dessert fork extended – and why humanity needed multiples of such implements, he could only vaguely understand – Merl pressed down on the cake with the thicker edge. He watched the cake compress at first, the body becoming increasingly dense as air pockets were crushed. Eventually, the caramelized sugar on top that formed the glaze gave way and the entire cake sprang back, his fork sliding through the fluffy body to meet the bottom with a slight chink.

A breath in took the sweetness of caramelized sugar, the slight hint of sour and tartness that came from this pineapple fruit and something richer and deeper, a layered taste that he had only recently begun to experience. Vanilla, a spice made from beans and added to so many desserts that most folk barely even noticed it. Everyday luxuries, that made their lives richer and more complex. A king's spice, so profusely utilized now to such great effect.

Flour, dark and rich in colour from the sugar and cinnamon and vanilla and who knew what else, separated. He repeated the process again, parting the square piece and extracting a small rectangular portion from the corner. Then a quick spearing with the fork, watching the cake bounce right back after each compression, before he inserted the whole piece into his mouth.

Not crumbly, not at all. Oh, some small shards of sugar had fallen aside, but the cake itself held together perfectly, not leaving idle crumbs behind. All the better, for as he placed it in his mouth, even his ability to process multiple flows of information was put on hold.

Rich, deep, complex taste exploded across his tongue.

Into his mouth.

Into his brain.

Caramelized sugar had its own taste, slightly burnt, slightly richer than the plain sugar used so commonly. That plain white sugar was certainly less complex than the berries and other fruits they had used to sweeten their meals in the past. Here, this sugar, caramelized and burnt, was no plain white one, lacking all subtlety, but something else, leaving a delicate smoky flavor in his mouth even as it paired with the tartness of the pineapple. He could sense hints of a sourness from the plant that should have been more pronounced, but was subdued by the heat. Instead, it paired well with the sugars, the unique taste of the fruit becoming more distinct.

That same taste, of the pineapple, was carried through into the flour itself. Subtler, though, as though the baker wanted to highlight another taste, the deepness of the vanilla, the heaviness of the flour and the... cream?

Merl shook his head, discarding thought as he chewed and took another bite. His was not a palate accustomed to a wide variety of spices, certainly not to the variations and the depth of flavor that were so common in the present day. If nothing else, the addition of salt in such vast quantities that it was laid out on the table for use by the common man was a vast departure. As was the presence of that black gold, the black pepper.

Largesse, everywhere. Nowhere more apparent than on the dinner table, such that even the peasantry might avail themselves of a meal that his King would not have been ashamed to grace his table with.

Hah! Ashamed.

He would have wept in delight. The man had always been free with his emotions, first to laugh, first to weep. His heart had been so great that friend and foe alike had marveled at it, though that same generosity of emotion had been his undoing.

And yet... and yet, none of his subjects would ever have wanted it otherwise. Even if he had wept when his wife betrayed him, even when his heart's other true love had been the one who broke their vows. Even when he had raised the banners and...

Oh, how his King would have loved this meal. One day, he would return.

Metal scraped against bare plate and Merl found his dish clean. He blinked, staring down at the empty dish, stained with droplets. He reached up and touched his face, surprised to find tears there. Surprised, even more, that Mika was silent.

Perhaps bureaucrats were not entirely unworthy, if they still understood grief.

"My lord?" Mika said, leaving the question unasked.

"Not lord. Never that..." Merl dried his face, unashamed. "An old memory, a good one. Though the regrets do not hurt less." He set the dessert fork down on the plate, touching the plate as he spoke, softly. "He would have liked this."

"Oh?"

"He was always interested in new experiences. New songs, new tales, new dishes..." Merl tilted his head up, then sideways out the door. He let out a breath, slowly. "He would find this new world... interesting."

"We've made many wonders," Mika said, carefully. "And many mistakes. But sometimes, it's hard to tell what is a mistake and what a wonder at first glance."

Merl snorted. "You wish me to move like the fae. Affecting little, touching nothing."

"We would ask that, yes. And perhaps, to speak with others. Who have been present more." Mika nodded to the kitchen where Mo Meng continued to work.

"I'll think about it." Merl furrowed his nose, and leaned forward. "Though, if I am not to create this money; how then would you recommend I exist in this twisted future?"

"Well, you see, we have a program..." Mika said, brightening a little as he fished inside his jacket for a card.

Stewing Thoughts

T he tiny figure that appeared at the edge of the barbecue grill, standing near where flames licked up occasionally, seemed entirely unconcerned by its imminent fiery demise or the radiant heat around its body. Then again, while a true sending, it lacked both physical nerves and the more sophisticated twistings of bound enchantments to allow its caster to feel what it did.

Unlike his present guise, the figure's appearance was reminiscent of its caster's older visage. White robes, knee-length and belted with a simple woven leather belt of multiple cords. Useful tools hung from it, hunting and skinning knives, a pouch for carrying twine and string and for storing what was gathered. A bronze sickle, hanging low down one side; well-worn but its edge sharp. The man was just as old, with a long, flowing white beard but a tonsure of a hairstyle, the hair shaved back. Most prominent was the oak staff, as the little figure leaned on it and peered up at Mo Meng as he cooked.

They stood in companionable silence for a time, as the chef flipped over some pieces and placed others, the rapidly diminishing pile of meat being warmed and cooked as he worked, chicken and barbecue ribs placed on plates and then set under warming lamps for Kelly to pick up. When he returned to the grill, only then did Merl speak.

"The mortal wants me to work for him."

"Not him. The government agencies," Mo Meng corrected idly. "There's always a lot of work to be done. You would not believe the number of old cursed grounds that have to be cleansed, hauntings to send back or even routine sweeps of buildings and personnel for undue supernatural influence." His lips twisted wryly. "Really, the last one is the most time-intensive."

"So, you've worked for them before."

"Not for many years, but yes. On occasion, when it mattered." He hesitated, then added, "Don't let them talk you into fighting any wars. Even when it matters..."

"About that, I know better." Something dark flickered through Merl's eyes. "It's why I am careful about where I visit. My father's influence in some places..."

"Important work, but let the children do it. It's better we stay away," Mo Meng said. "When we act, well..."

"Well, what?" Merl growled, thumping the end of the oak staff into the metal flooring.

Outside, the human Merl's face flickered, irritation leaking through. Not much, just a touch, but enough that Mika hesitated before he continued his explanation of what a pension and healthcare plan was. Not that he expected Merl to need one, or care that it was only available to government employees. However, the man had asked.

A short distance away, O continued to stare impatiently, arms crossed. Chastised several times, she had fallen into grumpy silence, her dessert lying half-untouched. An act that was generating more than a few scandalized looks from the regulars, most of all Eleanor, who licked her own red, red lips.

The babble of pleasant conversation, the smell of the meal, the slight chill in the air from the room's artificial air circulation, was all pleasant background noise to Mo Meng, like the slight, staticky hum of his wards or the gentle pressure of the lapping waves of energy. Out of it all, the burning pyre that was Merl was the disturbance, but his wards and the man's manners had brought it down to a comfortable inferno.

A nonsense phrase, if one had never stood before a burning city and seen the other.

"Do you know that most of the ingredients I buy are from locals?" Mo Meng said.

"No, why would I know that?" Merl replied, annoyed.

"No reason. Just that, to obtain the dozen-plus ingredients used today, I only had to use magic once. And that was mostly by choice. I could have acquired fresh pineapples another way, but wanted to speak to an old friend," Mo Meng said. "Heh. Old. They're oni. You know what that is?"

A shake of the head from Merl, an unsurprising admission. No reason for him to know Japanese demons, after all. His imprisonment had preceded the first contact.

"Japanese demons, like the ogres of your land. Strong, smart, loyal. Good front-line fighters, they used to come over the waters and lay waste to the countryside. The number I had slain..." A hand paused for a moment in the midst of flipping ribs around. It resumed, the motion not as smooth at first before evening out again. "Anyway, this clan.

They moved from Japan, over a century ago, to different lands. As sick of the killing as I was by then. Grow the best pineapples you can imagine, and all without much magic at all."

"So they changed." Merl snorted. "You make a poor bard, if you belabor your point."

"I do. I write even worse poetry, if you would like to hear some." Mo Meng's lips twitched. "Especially in Mandarin. But they changed, this world did. The goods we use, the world we have, it's all more closely tied together than ever. Or, perhaps, we see more of it now." A lip twitched. "Droughts in one nation, we hear about it. Realize it's going to affect wheat prices everywhere else. Or oil. Or..."

"So you think this world is too delicate for us to touch? Is that it?" Merl replied.

"No, we can do good. There's a lot who do, even our counterparts." Eyes sparkling with mischief, Mo Meng added. "Even those of the cross." He saw the tiny figure hunch down, that inferno of energy pulse, then still. "But they've learned to do it within the bounds of the world and the rules set up."

"No place for anarchy? For change, even when the system needs change?"

"The distribution of swords by strange women in lakes as a form of choice for governments has fallen out of favor." Mo Meng hesitated, then added. "You know what happened after. Why would they want to replicate that?"

"The Dark Ages."

"Only dark in certain countries and lands, but truly dark, yes." The chef shrugged. "If you want to indulge your other proclivities, there are countries where change, major change, has been enacted. Your father dips his fingers in them, constantly. Walk those streets for a while, and see what's it like."

"Not all stability is good."

"Not all things need to change." A slightly longer pause, before he added, "Or at least, not immediately. The world is more delicate than even we knew. Think long, decide slowly."

Disdain, now in Merl's voice. "Act seldom."

"But swiftly and decisively."

Merl raised an eyebrow at that, and Mo Meng shrugged. He was not against change. He saw what the other man did. He was just more wary, for he had made his own mistakes.

"And take this job offer?"

"At least look at their video presentations. It's not all wasted time."

He ignored the silent, hunched and white-robed figure as he finished another dozen plates. He eye-balled the quantities left, took a long gulp of water and refilled his cup before returning once more to his station. When he returned, the tiny figure sighed and straightened, breaking its silence.

"I will wait and watch and learn. But I make no promises about not acting. What they did to my land..."

"I know." Mo Meng sighed. "Why do you think I live here now?"

Not that this city was much better, nor what they had done to the natives of this land... Then again, existence was compromise. The longer he lived, the more starkly he felt that truth.

By the time he finished musing, mini-Merl had dispersed, leaving Mo Meng alone with his memories and his incomplete dishes.

Service Close

"Stop taking reservations," Mo Meng said to Kelly as she swept by to pick up a new set of plates. "We're out of the ribs after this batch. And have another half-dozen plates of the chicken."

Kelly would have complained, but she had been running – mostly metaphorically – for the last few hours. Her quiet evenings in the restaurant had faded, packed full with mundanes and magical beings. The regulars had come and gone, and even that strange older man, Merl, had left, his bill paid by the pair of agents. O had looked sullen, especially as she stuffed the bills he had conjured into her pocket. Thankfully, none of the mundanes had paid attention to any of that, though a few had sensed the change in atmosphere as Merl left.

Good riddance as far as she was concerned.

"I'll tell them," Kelly acknowledged before she rushed off to deliver the plates.

Water, a fresh napkin, a new fork for a dropped one, and then finally she got to the front doors. A few words became a longer conversation as she tried to appease the crowd before she had to leave, grabbing the credit card machine off a table and glancing at the total before slipping the extra merchant copy inside her apron. Back over two tables, drop the machine off after punching in the amount for three meals and then handing it over for the customer to finish up while she bussed the tables herself.

More water, thankfully the jug refilled by Mo Meng while she was away. She made it through another half-dozen tables, collecting requests and additions, before she was back, inputting desserts and completing calculations for bills from tables that were finished.

Plates kept being deposited in the kitchen, her eyes narrowing at the giant pile that had formed there. Without a dedicated dishwasher, it was only luck – and a little storage magic – that kept them able to offer new – and clean – dishes to their customers.

Forty-five minutes later; when the last of the customers trickled out, stuffed too full to be unhappy at the delay, did she close the door and slump against it gratefully. As she exhaled, a knock on the door made her tense.

"Yes?" she said, opening it once again.

"Party of three." The man who answered had his hand on the door, ready to push in.

"I'm sorry. We're closing early today. We're out of food."

"You're what?"

"Out of food. Sorry. Come again tomorrow?" she said with a smile.

"Nothing at all?" the man said, his voice growing a little desperate.

Foot behind the door, she smiled that customer-service smile that was all words and no warmth. "Nope, sorry!"

"Damn. Okay. Sorry for bothering you." He stepped back, then looked at the door and around. "You might want to have a sign saying that."

"Right. Yes. I'll get right on it!" she said. "Sorry again for the bother."

"It's fine." Another smile and then he turned around, releasing the door to speak to his companions. "Sorry guys, they're out. Maybe we should—"

Words cut off by the closed door, Kelly locked and slumped against it again. She hesitated, then stepped down behind the counter, scrabbling around for a pen and paper and tape before making her way back to the entrance to post a temporary CLOSED sign. By the time she got back, the trio had gone, leaving her to stare at the empty alleyway down which a pair of potential customers were striding determinedly.

Hurriedly closing the door, Kelly made sure it was locked. She was, once again, grateful to be Canadian. There might still be obnoxious customers, but they were certainly fewer in number than in the US. Breathing deeply, she descended to the restaurant, only to pause halfway down the stairs as Mo Meng exited his kitchen, helping bus the last of the tables.

"You don't need to do that," she cried.

"It's fine," Mo Meng said. "You know I used to do this before you came along, right?"

"Yes, but..."

"Then things got busy," Mo Meng said, musing out loud. "And you showed up and it made sense to hire you." A small smile. "You looked so lost, then."

"It was just after I got fired!" Kelly protested. "It was a rather bad day, eh."

"Not so bad, if it brought you here."

Those words made her hesitate, then a small smile bloom on her face. A small change, as her world and the past altered. Another smaller part of her wondered if perhaps some of her other bad days might not have been that bad.

"Been a while since we began. And now, we're running out food and there are more dishes than a family of brownies would care to do." He rubbed his chin. "Or, well, not."

"You thinking of hiring some brownies to be your dishwashers?" Kelly said, amused.

"Possibly. They're pretty good at their jobs, though they like variety more than routine," Mo Meng admitted, a smile dancing on his lips. "But I can put the word out."

"What about the, well, normal people?" She grabbed a cloth and began the process of wiping down tables, occasionally sweeping some of the crumbs to the floor. She'd sweep them all up later anyway.

"What about them?"

"Aren't brownies, like, small?"

"Glamour magic." He waved a hand towards the kitchen. "Lock it down within the kitchen, make them see what they expect to see."

"And what's that?"

"Someone slaving over the sinks, washing dishes." He chuckled, finished packing the dishes and brought them over to the kitchen sink. He eyed the pile, stepped back and pursed his lips.

"Are you going to do it?" she asked, a little eagerly. He so rarely did visible magic, especially around her. A big lack for a magical restaurant, she felt.

"I don't like using magic in the kitchen…"

"I know."

He sighed and rolled his shoulders. He looked around, at the grill that had to be cleaned – even if he'd done a few passes on it while he worked – and the pots and pans left behind, the garbage that had to be tossed, the floor that had to be swept and the knives to be sharpened. More counters and dishes and…

And he smiled.

What was the point of having magic if you didn't indulge, once in a while?

"Maybe just this once."

She grinned, leaving him to it as she returned to her own tasks. Magic, subtle magic, always fascinated her. As much as she'd like to watch wholeheartedly, she too had work to do. Still, she would peer over the counter as she worked. Watch as the dishes rose up in the air, soap bubbles and water sweeping over them, dirt and refuse sliding away. Dozens of magical hands, wiping and cleaning plates and depositing debris and foodstuff, knives and forks and spoons scrubbed and placed in the dryer.

Magic used for mundane tasks seemed all the more magical to Kelly. How often did one need a fireball to destroy an ogre? How often did you need to stop the sun from moving or create an impenetrable forest? On the other hand, dishes – well, dishes were something most people had to deal with on a daily basis.

Broom in hand, she swept the floors, starting from one corner and moving to the next. As she worked, she glanced into the kitchen as a song began, light and stringed. Not a violin or bass or guitar, but something a little louder, a little sharper.

"What is that?"

"A guzheng," Mo Meng replied; then, eyes glittering, he added. "Playing the Breath of the Wind."

A beat, then she laughed. "That's from a game, isn't it?"

"Yes," Mo Meng said, smiling a little. "It quite suits the instrument, don't you think?"

Silence descended on the room except for the sounds of their quiet industry and the light chords that filled the air. The music seemed to come from the air itself, filling the surroundings. They worked in companionable silence, Kelly idly noting how the air had cleared, grown purer with each moment, leaving nothing but the smell of old wood and bleach as she cleaned.

It did not take long for her to finish setting the chairs upright, to clear the front of the restaurant. When she was done, Mo Meng was still working. His reluctance to use magic other than for the dishes meant that he had significantly more cleaning to do.

Perched on the counter, she extracted the receipts and cash from the machine, doing a final count for the evening to separate out her tips. She glanced at Mo Meng as she did so, a pen and paper and her mobile phone by her side as she wrote down the details.

"Hey, do you pay taxes?" she said, curiously.

"I do." Mo Meng frowned, turning to her. "Why would you think I would not?"

"Magic restaurant."

He snorted. "I still make use of public services. Get deliveries by public roads, draw electricity, and shelter under the armies of this nation." He swiped at his nose with his shoulder where it had started itching, since his hands were covered with soap and oil. "One should not avoid paying a tithe just because one can. Lords are often jealous of their prerogatives."

Kelly stared at the tips she had noted and separated, and sighed. She knew he was right, but working in this industry, it was always tempting to underreport just a little. Certainly, a number of her friends did the same.

Mo Meng hid a smile by walking over to wash his hands, then exited the kitchen a moment later. That surprised Kelly; a glance within showed her there were still numerous surfaces to be washed down, oil traps to be cleared and the grill to be scraped after the warm water and soap had set a little more.

"I'm not done..." she said.

"I know." He took a seat and tilted his head to the side. "But we have to talk."

Eyes widening, Kelly searched her mind for what she might have done. In all her years, those were never words that led to a decent outcome. She blurted out, "I can quit the social media. I'm sorry, I didn't..."

"Not your fault." He sighed. "The magics were never meant to handle such proliferation of knowledge. Not when it is distributed across the world, held in so many devices. The few magics that might work..."

"There's magic that can work everywhere?"

"Yes." He shrugged. "It is not something I have experimented with, but there are spells that theoretically could work. Razorbeak's Scuttlebutt Destroyer. Su-Min Voice Ender of the Wind. But the casting would require…"

"Lily."

"Or someone of her status. More than that, the unforeseen consequences…" He shook his head. "No. A lesson already learned. This would always happen."

"I'm sorry."

"Nothing to be sorry about."

She hesitated then, when he fell silent. "Then?"

"If you're taking on more tasks, you should be paid for it. So. Hourly or salary?"

Kelly's jaw dropped, her mouth working speechlessly. Quite pleased at her shock, Mo Meng stood, and waved her back to her calculations.

"Later. Think about it for now and we'll talk after you're done."

Kelly snorted, and watched him leave with a self-satisfied smirk. For a man centuries old, he certainly seemed to delight in his little tricks.

Then, when his back was fully turned, she broke into a wide grin. Somehow, she didn't feel as stuck as before.

###

The End

**The Mo Meng will be back in Thaumaturgic
Tapas
Want to return to the Nameless Restaurant
already?
Visit www.mylifemytao.com/bonus-epilogues/
to read a short scene set after this book.**

The Hidden Wishes Series

Want to read more about Henry and Lily?

One faithful day Henry Tsien finds a briefcase and a ring within it. Within hours, his world has changed as a helpful jinn introduces him to a hidden world.

What can an old-school gamer given magic do in a world filled with age-old, hidden, supernatural creatures?

The Hidden Wishes series is an urban fantasy take on the GameLit genre. It is much lighter in terms of 'statistics' and its game system. This is the full trilogy of the series.

Books include:
A Gamer's Wish
A Squire's Wish
A Jinn's Wish

Enjoy the entire Hidden Wishes series in just one book!
https://readerlinks.com/l/3204832

Author's Note

Thank you for reading the second work in the Hidden Dishes series. I had, initially, planned for the work to be a one-off, a little diversion. However, Mo Meng and friends mugged me and gave me an entire arc that had to be written out.

So I now have a plan to write another three to five works in this series, covering various other denizens and newcomers to the world. I'm also working on in-between short stories, that will cover the introduction of some of our favorite regulars.

There's a definite arc meant for these novellas, but also, a desire to keep each work entirely separate. So readers can slip in, read a novella and not feel like they're missing out too much. Every story, self-contained but not.

I hope you enjoyed the series and the recipes. I'm testing out new ones for the next book, which I hope to have out a little faster.

As always, you should subscribe to my newsletter for further information about Hidden Dishes or other works by me.

~ Tao

If you haven't checked out the rest of the Hidden Wishes series please check out book 1 – A Gamer's Wish: https://books2read.com/u/3LKZMX

About the Author

Tao Wong is a Canadian author based in Toronto who is best known for his System Apocalypse post-apocalyptic LitRPG series and A Thousand Li, a Chinese xianxia fantasy series. His work has been released in audio, paperback, hardcover and ebook formats and translated into German, Spanish, Portuguese, Russian and other languages. He was shortlisted for the UK Kindle Storyteller award in 2021 for his work, A Thousand Li: the Second Sect. When he's not writing and working, he's practicing martial arts, reading and dreaming up new worlds.

Tao became a full-time author in 2019 and is a member of SF Canada, the Science Fiction and Fantasy Writers of America (SFWA) and ALLI.

Please check out A Gamer's Wish – book 1 of the Hidden Wishes Series.

For updates on the series and his other books (and special one-shot stories), please visit the author's website: www.mylifemytao.com

Subscribe to Tao's mailing list to receive exclusive access to short stories in the Thousand Li and System Apocalypse universes.

If you'd like to support Tao directly, he has a Patreon page - benefits include previews of all his new books, full access to series short stories, and other exclusive perks: www.patreon.com/taowong

Or visit Tao's Facebook Page: www.facebook.com/taowongauthor

For more great information about LitRPG series, check out these Facebook groups:

- LitRPG Society

www.facebook.com/groups/LitRPGsociety

- LitRPG Books

www.facebook.com/groups/LitRPG.books

About the Publisher

Starlit Publishing is wholly owned and operated by Tao Wong. It is a science fiction and fantasy publisher focused on the LitRPG & cultivation genres. Their focus is on promoting new, upcoming authors in the genre whose writing challenges the existing stereotypes while giving a rip-roaring good read.

For more information on Starlit Publishing, visit our website: www.starlitpublishing.com

You can also join Starlit Publishing's mailing list to learn of new, exciting authors and book releases.